A
Harlequin
Romance

NURSE'S DILEMMA

by

HILDA PRESSLEY

Harlequin Books

TORONTO • LONDON • NEW YORK • AMSTERDAM • SYDNEY • WINNIPEG

First published in 1965 by Mills & Boon Limited
under the title "The Greatest Gift"

© 1965 Hilda Pressley

SBN 373-00932-1

Halequin edition published July 1965
Reprinted 1965
Reprinted 1972
Reprinted 1976

Printed in Canada

CHAPTER ONE

ALYS had been in love with Richard Kent ever since the first day he came to St. Anne's six months ago as medical registrar. She remembered the day so well. She had just returned from a long convalescence after a particularly virulent type of pleurisy. Her first contact with him had been outside the station when the porter carrying her suitcase had thrust his way in front of Richard determinedly, claiming for her the only remaining taxi. She caught the swift reaction of anger on his face and the scorn in his dark eyes as he glanced significantly at her expensive fur coat—a present from her father—and the matching hat bought in London that morning.

She would have offered to share the taxi, but she felt the warm flush which suffused her cheeks and turned quickly away so that he should not see. The porter opened the door of the taxi and she stepped swiftly inside.

"Where to, lady?" the driver asked, opening his little window.

"St. Anne's Hospital, Alexandra Road," she told him, and they were off.

It was not until she came face to face with Richard the following day in the hospital's main corridor that she realised the man at the station had been Richard Kent, the new medical registrar. The only recognition he gave was a slight raising of his dark brows as he passed on his way, his stethoscope bulging out of his pocket, his long white coat open down the front as if he had not had time to fasten it. This might well have been

5

true, for the encounter, if such it could be called, took place at nine o'clock in the morning, much too early for doctors' rounds. Some emergency, no doubt, had taken him from his breakfast. Though the residents' breakfast was at eight, it was well known that many of them did not put in an appearance until much later. Not that the doctors and surgeons were wholly to blame. No ward Sister welcomed an M.O. before nine-thirty at the earliest. And as a general rule operations did not begin until that hour, either.

Her hand poised to knock at Matron's door, Alys gazed after him as he strode with firm tread in the direction of the medical wards. It was ridiculous to feel this way, she told herself, about a man to whom she had not even spoken. But as the days became weeks and the weeks months, she knew she had fallen in love with him.

Her interview with Matron had been quite significant. She, too, had started on a new job on the day the new medical registrar had taken up his post at St. Anne's.

"Well now, Sister," Matron had greeted her. "And how do you feel after your convalescence?"

"Oh, fine, Matron," Alys had assured her.

Matron smiled, as though that was exactly the answer she expected, but did not quite accept.

"I hardly think, though, Sister, that you're fit for the hectic life of a busy ward."

"Oh, but, Matron—"

Matron put up a hand. "Wait a moment, Sister, and I'll tell you what I have in mind. You, if I may say so, are one of our best nurses—a gold medallist of whom I and St. Anne's can be justly proud. I have always found you everything to be desired. You're fully trained and have had experience in every department. You have been one of the few people—both as a student nurse and as a trained nurse—that I could call on so often to act as relief. You have always been so adaptable." She broke off and smiled again. "What I am offering you, Sister, what I am asking you to do is to join my administrative staff."

Alys's eyes widened. "Your administrative staff!"

Matron eyed her keenly. "There's a lot to be said for administrative work, Sister. I daresay you've never considered that aspect of nursing. Good nurses often don't. They're dedicated to the bedside of the patient, forgetting that only the dedicated nurse makes a good administrator. No one can pass on to others what is not in them to pass on, and I feel I owe it to both patients and nurses in my care to make certain of having the right people as my deputies."

Alys swallowed hard. "Matron, I'm overwhelmed by your good opinion of me—and by your generous offer. I—I never even dreamed of such a thing."

"To my mind, you're absolutely the most ideal person," Matron said determinedly. "Especially for the particular duties I have in mind for you."

"What are they, Matron?" Alys asked weakly.

"Primarily the duties of Home Sister. And, of course, you will relieve the second deputy Matron on round duties. But your main concern will be the well-being of the nurses. You're young, you've already done a spell as Home Nurse, haven't you?"

"It seems a good many years ago now, Matron."

"Nevertheless, you did it, and I think you'll have just the right touch with our young student nurses. I can tell you frankly, Sister, now that the people concerned are no longer here. Sister Henderson was too strict— I'm sure I don't need to tell you that. You were a student nurse yourself in her day. On the other hand, Sister McIntyre was far too lax. She let the nurses run riot. What I want is somebody who will strike the right balance between the two. I don't want somebody who will try to enforce too many petty restrictions on the nurses—and I'm quite sure they don't either. On the other hand, they don't want to be spoon-fed, but cared for, without letting them do just as they like. Above all, I feel the Home Sister should be someone in whom the nurses can confide or go to for advice, someone they can respect. In other words, an elder sister rather than a second 'mum'."

"It sounds a tall order, Matron," Alys said doubtfully. "I don't think I could live up to it."

What Matron had said about the last two Home Sisters was true. How well she remembered Sister Henderson, who would even open nurses' drawers to see whether they were tidy, and if she considered a bed had not been made properly by its owner, would strip it and leave the bedding in a bundle and tip up the mattress. Or if she suspected a party was going on in someone's bedroom would burst in without ceremony and break it up, especially if the hour was what she considered late. These and many other meannesses. As to Sister McIntyre, she had not cared either about the nurses' welfare or the state of the Nurses' Home. But Alys loved nursing, and this was tantamount to giving it up.

"I'm quite sure you'd be an improvement on both," Matron said firmly, adding, with remarkable insight : "You mustn't feel as though you're giving up practical nursing, you know. Among so many nurses there's nearly always one or other of them off sick. And of course you'll be doing ward rounds quite often. At least give it a trial, will you?"

All at once, the idea appealed to her. "You're very kind, Matron. Yes, I will give it a trial—and thank you."

"Good. Now. As you may know we have a new

medical registrar in place of Dr. Benton, and he has taken over as the nurses' panel doctor. I wouldn't be surprised if a number of nurses who have doctors outside transfer to him. He's young—at least in comparison with Dr. Benton—and quite attractive in a rugged kind of way. As a matter of fact there are two nurses in sick bay at this very moment, so you'll probably meet him some time during the day."

The two nurses in question were recovering from influenza. Not knowing exactly what time to expect Dr. Kent, Alys went about her other duties. It was actually late in the afternoon when he came. Alys went along to sick bay to make tea for her two patients and discovered him already there chatting to them.

He turned as she entered and gave her a hard stare. She sensed antagonism in him and her mind flew back to the incident of the taxi. Obviously, he had not yet forgiven her that. He waited for her to speak.

"Dr. Kent?" she enquired. "I'm Sister Newton."

His dark brows lifted slightly. "Home Sister?"

"That is correct. I hope you haven't been here long. I was not sure what time to expect you."

"I'll give you advance notice in future."

She detected sarcasm in his voice, but decided to ignore it.

"That would be best, if you don't mind, Doctor, then I can be on hand to attend you."

He made no reply. He turned to the first nurse and asked how she was feeling.

"Much better now, thank you, Doctor," came the reply coupled with a look which was frankly interested in the new M.O.

Alys handed him the nurse's temperature chart. He glanced at it, then took out his stethoscope and made the most thorough examination.

"Hm. Chest seems all right. Another week in bed,

Sister, a good nourishing diet, then a fortnight's convalescence."

He repeated both the examination and the prescription for the other nurse, then nodded to them and left them with broad smiles at the prospect of a fortnight's sick leave. Alys escorted him to the door of the Home.

"I suppose you think I've been over-generous with those two?" he demanded without looking at her.

"No," she said on a note of surprise. "Generous, perhaps, but not excessively so. After all, influenza is both weakening and depressing."

"I'm glad to hear you say so." He looked at her then from under his dark brows. "What, if I may ask, is someone as young as you—and obviously a good nurse —doing wasting her time in a position like Home Sister? Surely it's a job for either the middle-aged or work-shy?"

She felt herself colouring. "I'm afraid I can't agree with you, Dr. Kent, and I feel you're entirely wrong to jump to conclusions. I'll see to it that your instructions with regard to the nurses are carried out."

Again, that uncompromising stare before he hurried down the broad steps and strode in the direction of the hospital wards.

She put the rapid beating of her heart and the tears which pricked her eyes down to her own physical weakness following her illness, but she knew in her heart it was much more personal than that.

All this had happened six months ago, and since that time there had been scarcely a minute in which he had not been somewhere in her mind. His tall figure striding along the main corridor or across the quadrangle, his uncompromising stare, his way of saying exactly what he liked, and which never failed to spark anger in her.

Naturally, he very soon acquired something of a

reputation in the hospital. He was a person to be reckoned with, to be admired and to be respected. But to Alys, he remained a person to be loved long after she had recovered from the ravages of her illness.

She came to love her job as Home Sister, caring for the young student nurses, nursing them through their winter ills. She soon discovered that—like those of her own student days—they would do anything rather than go off sick. Usually, it was left to a friend to report them and to Alys herself to bundle them into bed and "send for Dr. Kent," whose list of nurse panel patients had increased enormously.

"I'm sure it's not because of his bedside manner," sniffed Miss Tindall, first deputy Matron.

Alys smiled. "I don't think a bedside manner would go down at all with the student nurses of today. They prefer sincerity to a false sort of patting of the head."

"He seems very fond of handing out sick leave, at any rate. No wonder they're all fighting to get on his panel. He certainly is a nurse's man, but there are a good many of the Sisters who don't like him, I can tell you."

A doctor or surgeon who was popular with the nurses was rarely liked by the senior staff—a situation which probably had its roots in a man who has himself suffered at the hands of some martinet of a ward or departmental Sister, and who in consequence becomes the champion of the student nurse and the antagonist of the senior.

After a while Richard joined the hospital social club, and it was at the initial dance of the tennis section that Alys had her first social contact with him. He came and stood before her, a mocking light in his eyes.

"Ah, Sister Newton. May I have the honour?"

By now, they had sparred on so many occasions, it seemed natural to continue their sparring even on the dance floor.

"The pleasure, you mean," she retorted. "At least, I hope that's what it will be."

His lips twitched into a smile. "We shall just have to see, won't we?"

As she had really expected—since he appeared to do all things well—he was a very good dancer. He had a good sense of rhythm, was easy to follow even in the more intricate steps. Obviously, he felt the same way about her dancing.

"Where did you learn to dance so well?" he asked. "Not here in Nedaby, I'll be bound."

"And why not?" she challenged.

She found she had had to adopt this prickly attitude towards him as a sort of defence against her love for him. Not for a moment must he guess how she felt about him.

But tonight he appeared in the mood to flirt. Holding his head back as they danced, he looked into her eyes, a smile of amusement curving his lips.

"When you're angry—which I must admit seems to be most of the time—your eyes spark with real fire." His smile broadened. "Eyes are interesting, don't you think? Yours are the colour of amber flecked with green —like a tiger's."

Her cheeks flamed. "Don't be ridiculous, Dr. Kent!"

His black brows shot up revealing his own deep blue eyes. "Oh, Richard, please," he mocked. "Let's not be so formal."

She compressed her lips tightly in a mixture of pain and anger. Why must he be so sarcastic the whole time? Why couldn't he be just ordinarily friendly? The only thing for her to do was treat him in the same vein.

"Oh, let's not," she said airily, though the effort cost her a great deal. "You may call me Alys."

"Alice?" he repeated in a surprised voice. "That's a simple, old-fashioned name. I like it."

She gathered her defences more tightly around her. "I hope this doesn't disappoint you—but it's spelt A-l-y-s—not, in what I expect is the old-fashioned way."

"Hm! I might have known it. Alice spelt the old way would be much too ordinary for you, wouldn't it?"

"I didn't choose it myself," she retorted. "People rarely do choose their own names, you know."

"No, but they often change the spelling."

"Well, I can assure you I didn't!"

He laughed. "All right, all right! Calm down. There's no need to get so het-up."

"Really!" She took an angry breath. "You make the most odd insinuations and expect me not to be annoyed."

The music stopped and there was scattered applause as they stood and faced each other, she with anger still in her eyes, he blandly smiling. She must be crazy to love this man! Why did she? she fumed inwardly. Then the music started again and he said, this time without a trace of sarcasm:

"I hope you're not too angry to dance the encore with me—Alys. It's a very nice name whichever way it's spelt, and I didn't mean to insinuate anything." With a smile which was oddly appealing, he held out his hand.

Her anger vanished like snow before the sun, and she put her hand in his once more. For a short while neither spoke. Alys was conscious of her hand in his, his arm half around her waist, and for a moment she savoured his nearness, then she felt the pressure of his hand and the arm around her waist tightened. She resisted in a sort of panic.

"I don't care to be held too tightly—if you don't mind," she said in a voice which closely resembled his for sarcasm.

His hold loosened immediately. "I beg your pardon," he said with exaggerated politeness. "Quite unintentional, I assure you. Perhaps you'd prefer to sit the rest of the dance out."

"I really don't mind one way or the other," she told him swiftly.

"Very well." He manoeuvred his way to the edge of the dancing area and led her to a seat. "As my company appears to irk you, I'll leave you in peace," he said, and vanished without another word.

The next time she saw him he was dancing with Olivia Longford, a glamorous young Sister of one of his wards. Alys glanced around the room and caught the eye of Ben Chalmers, the senior surgical registrar to whom Olivia was once engaged. Ben rose and came to ask her to dance.

"Haven't seen much of you since you came back from your convalescence and got yourself promoted. How are you now? Like your new job?"

"I'm fine," she told him, "and quite settled in looking after the nurses. I was dubious at first. I thought I'd miss the patients, but I like it now."

He thought for a moment. "Well, of course, you're still concerned with *people*, aren't you? You've got a responsibility towards them, even though they're not sick. Maybe that's the thing that satisfies you."

"Yes, I suppose you're right. I hadn't thought of it in that way."

She liked Ben Chalmers. He was the quiet, gentle type with a way of running his fingers through his fine, light brown hair. She had never known him to be rude to any nurse, but he would quietly and firmly insist in having things done his way. When he had first come to St. Anne's some of the Sisters tried to take advantage of his quiet courtesy, but they had learned sooner than they expected that when he asked for a thing to be done he meant it to be carried out. What a contrast between him and Richard Kent, she thought. She wondered whether he was still in love with Olivia. She had never heard the reason for their break-up. It had happened while she had been away, and by the time she came back the affair had been stale news.

"I must say you're looking much better these days. In fact there's something different about you altogether," Ben's voice broke into her thoughts.

She laughed. "Really?" She thought it likely that, at one time, he had eyes for no one else except Olivia. "Are you sure it's not you who's more observant?"

"Possibly, though I doubt it." She saw his gaze wander to where Olivia and Richard were dancing, and her own heart gave a nasty little twist as they obviously shared some joke. "It's getting rather hot in here," Ben said suddenly. "Let's have a drink, shall we? Unless, of course, you'd really prefer to finish the dance."

She shook her head. "A drink would be very welcome. I agree with you. It is getting rather unbearable in here."

Unbearable, not because of the heat, but because Richard was obviously finding Olivia's company so much more enjoyable than he had her own, because Olivia was so attractive, so much more likely to win Richard's love.

Ben led her to a seat in the nurses' sitting room, set apart for the evening as a sitting-out room, then went to get drinks. Alys watched him vaguely, her mind still occupied with thoughts of Richard.

She really would have to do something about her feelings for Richard, she told herself firmly. Obviously he was not attracted to her in the least. She must try to stop thinking about him, nip this love she thought she had for him ruthlessly in the bud. It couldn't be the real thing, anyway. She barely knew him. It just couldn't be any more than a superficial attraction.

She put a little extra brightness in her smile as Ben returned with their drinks.

"Thank you, Ben, this is very nice of you. Perhaps now the tennis season is beginning we shall see a little more of each other."

He looked at her with a smile of pleasure. "I hope so, too. What with your pleurisy and my—er—preoccupation with Olivia, we almost lost touch. Odd how you can do that, working in the same hospital."

"I was—sorry to hear about you and Olivia."

He smiled ruefully. "It's better to find out before marriage rather than after that you haven't really got so much in common, after all. Getting to know a person is quite a lengthy business, really. A period of engagement is a very good thing. You can't hope to get to know each other as well as you do in marriage, of course, but at least you get some idea. It would be better if there were more broken engagements and fewer broken marriages."

He was right, of course. "You—don't believe in love at first sight, then?"

He shook his head. "I don't think it is love, really. It's just an attraction, isn't it? Sometimes it comes to something, of course. But more often than not it's just a transient thing, and I should think that unless you get to know each other fairly quickly, such a so-called love would die a natural death, anyway. I think love is more like a plant, something that grows rather than just happens, and much of the growth goes on underground before it shows on top at all."

Alys eyed him with a new interest. "I think you've got something there."

All at once, she felt he would be a very nice person to get to know. She had always liked him from what little she knew of him. She had worked with him in theatre and the surgical wards, and once or twice he had asked her out to dinner. Then his name had begun to be linked with that of Olivia, and the next thing was, they were engaged.

"Do you live in, Alys, or not?" Ben was asking. "I know you used to share a flat with Sister Robins, but she's left now, hasn't she?"

She nodded. "I *am* living in at the moment. I've got Home Sister's bedroom and sitting room. But I let the flat go when Celia left. I think I might look out for another place, though. It's not right to be on top of the job the whole time."

But Ben was looking across the room to where Richard and Olivia were just coming through the door.

"Would you like to dance again, Alys?" he asked.

Obviously, he still felt something for Olivia, she thought, as she rose to her feet and accompanied him back to the ballroom.

CHAPTER TWO

MATRON did one of her periodic rounds of the Nurses' Home the following day. Alys had asked the cleaners to leave all the doors of the nurses' rooms open—except where its occupant was off duty—so that Matron could see inside without having to open each door. The nurses' rooms received a thorough cleaning once a week, the cleaners preferring to work in pairs, doing one corridor a day.

"Some of the nurses are not very tidy, Sister," Matron remarked as she caught glimpses of lumpy beds, shoes and stockings and other garments strewn about the floor, and in more than one case, a bed unmade entirely. "What line do you adopt with that sort of thing?"

Alys hesitated. "I—have no particular line, Matron. A nurse's own room is the only means of privacy she has. Some are naturally more tidy than others, of course, but I don't comment unless I feel it's absolutely necessary. If I happen to go into a nurse's room while she's there and the room is excessively untidy, I laugh and make some comment in a friendly way to show her I've noticed. And if, of course, a room is so untidy that the women can't clean it properly I wait until the nurse comes over for coffee or lunch, then ask her to tidy it."

For a moment Matron made no comment, and Alys feared she might not approve of her method—or lack of it. But to her surprise, Matron said after a moment's thought :

"I'm sure you're right, Sister. After all, the majority of our nurses come from good homes, and we must allow them some freedom and individuality away from the wards. Anyhow, I suppose untidy bedrooms are the least of your worries, aren't they? What about the playing of record players and transistors in their rooms —and coming in late at night?"

"Well—about late nights, Matron. What I try to do is watch the nurses' *health*. That way, they feel I care about them as people rather than about their morals. If a nurse isn't looking well and I feel she's having more late nights than is good for her I have a chat with her. I'm getting to know the nurses pretty well now. I know who has a regular boy friend, what kind of things they do in their off-duty, who their particular friend is among the nurses and so on. As to record players and transistors, I find they deal with each other adequately without my interference. They tick each other off soon enough if somebody is making too much noise. Usually, of course, they join in together—pool their records, so that their direct neighbours are often in on the same pop session. Not all of them can afford their own record player or transistor."

Matron nodded. "I see. Well, I'm glad you know how to deal with them, Sister. Most of them belong to the hospital jazz club, I suppose?"

"Many do, Matron, but it may surprise you to know that almost an equal number belong to the music club —the classics section."

"I suppose they do, really. One tends to think that all teenagers are pop mad."

Alys laughed. "Many of the nurses belong to both sections, Matron. I do myself."

But Matron's mind had switched to something else. "There'll be a new batch of student nurses coming in from the P.T.S. next Monday, Sister. How is the vacant room situation? Two more staff nurses are going to live out, beginning from Saturday, so that will leave you two more."

'They discussed the room question as Matron progressed from corridor to corridor of the four-storey building. On the top floor the night nurses had their rooms, and directly beneath these were the nurses' library and reading room, the writing room and a small chapel which had come to be known as the Quiet Room.

"Yes. Well, everything appears satisfactory, thank you, Sister," Matron said as Alys escorted her to the door at the end of the round. "Was there anything else?"

"Only that I'm thinking of living out again myself, Matron, if that's all right with you."

"Perfectly, Sister. You can still use the Home Sister's sitting room. There won't be any point in putting anyone in those rooms. We can keep the bedroom in case of emergency—though whatever emergency I can't imagine."

Preparing for the new batch of student nurses who were passing out of the training school kept Alys quite busy during the next few days. It was the custom—and a very good one, she considered—to put all of them together on one corridor. Those Sisters who preferred to live in had a special corridor with bed-sitting rooms, and Alys liked to put staff nurses together, too, though the majority of those who lived in were student nurses. This strategic placing of staff entailed some moving around at times like these, also gave plenty of room for speculation as to what the new nurses would be like. So far, she had been lucky in that all the nurses in her care had been average to good in their general behaviour. But at all events it would be an added interest, getting to know somewhere in the region of twenty-five new personalities.

She had not seen Richard since the night of the dance. At the present moment there were no nurses in the sick bay. It was now early June and the season for influenza and other winter ills long past. This was the season of tennis tournaments and cricket matches, and on Saturday there was a hospital tennis tournament, followed by a special late tea in the Nurses' Home and dancing in the evening. Alys had put her name down to play and had noticed that both Richard and Ben had also. The draw for partners was usually done on the day of the tournament.

With a thrill of excitement she tried to suppress at the thought that she would be seeing Richard again, or even be lucky enough to draw him as a partner, Alys changed after lunch on Saturday into white shorts and a shirt and joined the rest of the staff gathering at the tennis courts. But Richard wasn't even there. Ben strolled up to her immediately.

"Have you drawn for your partner yet?" she asked.

He nodded. "Believe it or not, I've drawn to partner you. Hope you're as pleased as I am."

She stifled the swift disappointment she felt. It was silly, she told herself. She probably wouldn't have drawn to play Richard, anyway.

"Of course I'm pleased," she told Ben. "We might even win. You won several times last year, didn't you?"

"So did you. So it's probably in the bag."

She smiled then. "We haven't seen what our new—or at any rate, new to tennis—medical registrar can do yet, this being the first tournament."

"Is he playing?"

"His name's down. Maybe he's held up somewhere."

Some of the heats were already being played, and as soon as they could Ben and Alys began to play, too. It was a beautiful day. It felt good to be playing again, good to be fit, too, after her illness. She and Ben won their three sets, and when they came off the court Richard had arrived and was chatting to Olivia. Alys thought they seemed to be on rather special terms and wondered, with a pang, whether they had been out together. It was more than likely. She couldn't help thinking how well suited they were. Both were tall and dark and looked particularly striking in white, and each had a ready wit which matched the other's.

Richard turned as Ben and Alys approached, his look flicking from one to the other, then coming back to rest on Alys, a mocking light in his eyes with which she was becoming very familiar.

"Well, well! If it isn't the reverend Home Sister. I hardly recognised you in your tennis rig."

She affected a blank stare, then a look of surprise. "Dr. Kent, isn't it? I'm so sorry. If I'd thought you'd have any difficulty at all, I'd have chosen to play in uniform. But we all look so different in mufti, don't we? I hardly recognised you at first, either. You look so handsome in white. But may I put you right, if you don't mind, Dr. Kent?" she went on with mock politeness. "I'm Sister of the Nurses' Home, not the Reverend Mother of a convent."

As she was speaking his eyes had become increasingly wider and there was the suggestion of a smile about his mouth.

"No? I beg your pardon. A natural mistake."

"Now then, you two!" came from the resident gynaecologist who was taking down the scores and arranging the matches. "No scrapping except on the courts. Sister Newton, do you feel equal to another match right away or would you rather take a breather first?"

"No, no, I'm quite fit, thanks," she said quickly, as she caught a look of impatience on the face of Olivia Longford.

"Oh, really, Lewis!" Olivia said to the gynaecologist. "Let's play someone else, for goodness' sake. I'd hate to take unfair advantage of Sister Newton, and I can't stand all this messing about."

"I really think you should take a rest between matches, Alys," Ben put in. "Besides, I don't know about you, but I could do with a drink."

At this, Alys saw a speculative look in Richard's eyes, and he seemed about to say something else, but Lewis Grainger spoke first.

"All right. Sister Longford and Dr. Kent will play Nurses Gregory and Nash. They're coming off the court now."

Ben took Alys's arm and led her to a deck chair, then brought a couple of glasses of lemonade.

"Ah, that's better," he said, sitting down beside her. "You know, you mustn't let somebody like Kent goad you into overtaxing your strength. You're pretty fit at the moment, I daresay, but it doesn't do to use up too much energy all at once. Two matches in succession is much too strenuous for you. Come to that, it is for anyone. We're not exactly professionals."

She smiled. "It's nice of you to be so concerned."

He sipped his drink thoughtfully for a moment. "You and Kent do seem to spark each other off, don't you?"

She fiddled with the straws in her glass. "Yes, I—I suppose we do. I don't know why it is, but he just gets under my skin."

She knew why, of course, but had said what she felt was expected of her.

"I don't blame you, hearing some of the things he says. But you seem to hold your own with him pretty well, anyway. When you're ready we'll go and play another of our matches, shall we?"

This sparring in verbal battle between Richard and herself became almost a habit. Every time they met they exchanged mild insults and sarcastic comments. Olivia and he had been drawn to partner each other, and inevitably, before the afternoon was over, the two played against Ben and herself.

Stung by some of his remarks, Alys was determined to win, and sent slashing shots over the net.

"Look, what are you trying to do? Maim me for life?" he called out once as a ball hit him squarely in the midriff.

"No such luck," she answered. "Anyway, you're supposed to use your racket to stop the balls, not your stomach."

Ben and she won the set, six-four, four-six, seven-five. They also won the next set in the semi-finals and went on to win the tournament.

As the umpire gave the score Ben dropped his racket and swung Alys round off her feet.

"Well done, Alys! You've played magnificently."

"No, no, it was you. You pulled us up every time with your service."

Everyone else crowded round to offer congratulations, including Richard. But his voice was loaded with sarcasm.

"Congratulations, both of you," he said. "You were perfect partners in every way."

"Thank you, Dr. Kent, thank you," she retorted. "How absolutely right you are."

"Of course, if you hadn't practically knocked me out—"

"You'd have won, I suppose?"

"Now, break it up, you two," called out Lewis Grainger. "You've all got just a quarter of an hour in which to change for tea."

It was odd, this continual banter between them. Richard kept it up throughout the entire evening. Sometimes she got quite a kick out of it, at other times she felt hurt by some of the things he said.

"Of course, in your job, you'll have plenty of energy

for tennis, won't you?" he said once. "Tell me, Alys, just what do you do with yourself all day?"

She drew an angry breath. "Sister Newton, if you please. If you must know, I feed my cats and sit and do my knitting."

He grinned. "Just as I thought—*Sister*. You know, I don't know how you can do it. Wasting your time over there when you should be nursing the sick."

"I'm caring for those who nurse the sick. Surely that's very necessary?"

"Yes, but it's hardly a job for a trained nurse, is it?"

"At times, yes. At others, it just happens to be the job for me."

After this conversation he called her "Sister Newton" with infuriating frequency, giving the title exaggerated emphasis.

"You're pretty insufferable, aren't you?" she was driven to say to him towards the end of the evening.

His dark brows shot up. "Am I? Well, if I may so say, you're not doing so badly yourself. You've insulted me right, left and centre and baited me unmercifully. What did you expect me to do? Take it all with a smile and a 'thank you'?"

"You're the one who has usually begun it."

He shook his head emphatically. "Oh no! In any case—"

But she never knew what he was going to say. They were dancing a Paul Jones, and the music changed.

As she was dancing the last waltz with Ben, he said to her: "Will you come out and have dinner with me one evening soon?"

"I'll be glad to, Ben," she told him warmly. "I have a long evening next Wednesday, if that's any use to you."

He said it would do fine. "I shall be looking forward to it. I'll wait for you in the car park around six. O.K.?"

She nodded. It was nice to hold a normal conversation with someone after so much of Richard and his aggravating sarcastic comments.

Yet, she thought, her lips curving into an amused smile as she prepared for bed later, it had been fun. In a way, she had enjoyed sparring with him. Sadly, however, she had to admit that, at best, this savoured of a brother-and-sister relationship rather than the one she would have liked. Why was it that the thing one longed for was always out of reach, while the less desirable was usually close to hand? She liked Ben. Of course she did. But if only he were Richard.

The new batch of student nurses moved into the Home on Sunday evening. Alys made out a list of the nurses, and alongside each name placed the number of her room. This she pinned on the notice board in the vestibule, also printed each nurse's name on a small card to place into the name-holders on each room door.

There was a public telephone on the ground floor for the use of the nurses, and during the evening Alys answered its ring to discover it was a caller for one of the new nurses, Edna Farrel.

"Will you hang on a moment, please? I'll go and find her for you."

She put down the receiver and had a quick look at her list, then went and knocked on the door.

"Nurse Farrel, telephone for you."

The door opened, and at the same time a nurse appeared from the next room, too. Alys looked from one to the other.

"You're Nurse Farrel, aren't you?" she said to the nurse who had appeared from the room next door.

She was a tall, fair-haired girl with a sullen expression which looked permanent.

"Yes. Did you say there was a telephone call for me?"

Alys looked at her. "You're in the wrong room, Nurse. You, too," she added turning to the other girl.

"We changed over. Nurse Farrel—"

"Then you had no business to without my permission. I won't make you change back again, but will you change the name cards over, please?"

"If that *was* a phone call for me—" Nurse Farrel said in an insolent tone, stepping out into the corridor.

"Yes, Nurse, it was."

The nurse brushed past her rudely, muttering something about "petty restrictions."

"Nurse Farrel!" Alys called after her sharply.

But though the girl must have heard, she paid no attention, but continued on her way along the corridor to the telephone. Alys turned to the other nurse.

"Understand this, Nurse Goodall. I must be able to find any one of you nurses quickly, and if everyone began changing rooms it would be chaotic. There are very few restrictions put upon you, but I have my job to do just the same as you will have yours when you start on the wards. We don't have a lot of rules and regulations in the Home, but there must be some for the good of all. Remember that. If there's anything you're not happy about or if there's any way in which I can help you, you have only to come and see me. You know where my office and sitting room are."

"Yes, Sister. I'm sorry. I didn't realise."

Alys smiled then. "That's all right, Nurse. Good luck tomorrow on your first day."

"Thank you, Sister."

Alys retraced her steps. Nurse Farrel had probably been the instigator of the move. Her manner just now had been both insolent and discourteous. It looked as though there might be trouble with this nurse. She rounded the corner and spoke to the girl as she passed the telephone.

"Nurse Farrel, when you've finished on the phone, will you come to my office, please?"

She received a stare, but no reply. Troubled, Alys went to her office. Just what did one do with such blatant rudeness? Obviously, the girl had a chip on her shoulder. There were some people who disliked all or any authority, who considered courtesy to be a sign of softness or submissiveness. But courtesy was not a thing one could enforce. It sprang naturally from inward happiness, from a normal adjustment to life, an ordinary liking for one's fellows. So far, there had been a mutual respect between Alys and the nurses—in some instances, even friendship.

She waited in the office for quite some time, but Nurse Farrel did not put in an appearance. What did one do with out-and-out defiance? The girl had come through preliminary training school all right. If she went on in this way when she began working on the wards, she would find herself in serious trouble.

Alys fought down a natural annoyance. Why did a person defy authority in this way? Too much parental discipline? One wouldn't have thought there was such a thing these days. Perhaps the girl had no parents. There was usually some reason for this kind of behaviour. The thing was : what was she to do about it? How to deal with Nurse Farrel? It was an hour ago since she had asked the girl to come to her office. Alys decided to give her the benefit of the doubt and conclude she had not heard her. She went and knocked at the girl's door, and hearing a voice call out, "Come in," she opened it. Nurse Farrel was lying on the bed reading a magazine. She made no attempt to move as Alys entered.

"I don't think you heard me, Nurse. I asked you to come to my office. I want to talk to you."

The blue eyes went insolently back to her magazine. "I'm off duty."

Alys looked at her for a moment and forced down a desire to snatch the magazine out of the girl's hand.

"I'm not asking you to work, I know you're off duty. I must remind you, Nurse, that you are in training, and while you're in the Nurses' Home, I am responsible for you, and I am Matron's deputy."

"Don't we get any freedom at all from authority?"

"Certainly you do. The same kind of freedom any normal citizen would get wherever he or she happened to be. Even if you were in an hotel and you were asked —not told—to go to the manager's office, that he had something to say to you, you would surely go, even if only out of courtesy? I am asking you now, Nurse Farrel, will you please come to my office?"

"Can't you say what you've got to say now, here?"

"No, Nurse. Certainly not while you're lying there on the bed. I don't think you can have any idea how rude you're being."

At this, Nurse Farrel flung her magazine aside with an exaggerated sigh. Alys moved towards the door.

"Don't come to the office, Nurse, come to my sitting room in about five minutes' time, and we'll have a cup of tea together."

Alys felt it was the only thing to do if she were going to win the girl's confidence and remove any idea that she was going to be "on the carpet." But if Alys expected any humility or softening of Nurse Farrel's attitude there was very little evidence of any as she knocked on the Home Sister's sitting room door a short while later. Alys had made the tea and was just setting out cups and saucers.

"Ah, come in and sit down, Nurse."

There was no polite "thank you" from the girl. She sat down, saying nothing, but Alys noticed the way she glanced around the room and the expression of sullen resentment on her face.

Alys poured out the tea and asked her to help herself to sugar.

"Are you looking forward to starting on the wards tomorrow, Nurse?" she asked.

A shrug from Nurse Farrel. Alys felt near-despair wash over her. There must be some way of reaching this girl.

"Nurse Farrel," she said evenly, "let's try to come to an understanding, shall we? As I explained to Nurse Goodall, there are not a lot of rules or restrictions in the Home, certainly not 'petty ones' as you insinuated when I spoke to you downstairs. I have to know where all the nurses are, in case any of you are needed in a hurry. Actually, there are no rules, as such. It's just that I am in charge here, in the same way as a ward Sister is in charge of the wards. All that is required of you when you are in the Nurses' Home is that you behave with the same courtesy and consideration your own family would expect of—"

She broke off suddenly, as the nurse put down her cup and saucer with a clatter and sprang to her feet, her eyes gleaming with anger and resentment.

"I don't want a lecture with a cup of tea thrown in, thanks!"

Alys rose to her feet, her own anger only just under control.

"Nurse, I will not tolerate such rudeness. I didn't have to give you a cup of tea. You could have had the 'lecture' as you call it, without, and I would have been quite justified in reporting your rudeness to Matron. I am on duty, even if you aren't, and when I am I expect, for one thing, to be addressed as Sister, in the same way that I address you as Nurse. There's simply no excuse for your attitude, whatever the circumstances or wherever you are. You're just about the rudest person I have ever met in my life!"

But before Alys had finished speaking, Nurse Farrel was halfway to the door, and without saying another word, she wrenched it open and went out, leaving it wide open behind her.

Alys heaved a heavy sigh and went to close it, then sat down feeling ragged, and conscious of a complete sense of failure. She felt she had just had to make a stand, yet what had it achieved? Off duty, the girl seemed absolutely determined to do and say what she liked, including being downright rude if she felt like it. Alys poured herself another cup of tea and worried the matter, wondering whether she should have adopted a different approach. What was biting the girl? What had made her so angry? The mention of her own family? Perhaps that was it. Perhaps she had no family. Alys determined to ask Matron about the girl, if she could do so without giving the impression she was complaining about her.

There was a knock at the door, and Alys called out "Come in," hoping it would be Nurse Farrel coming back to offer her apologies. But she was disappointed. It was one of the second-year nurses.

"Yes, Nurse, what is it?" she asked.

"It's Nurse Petch, Sister. She's got an awful pain. I think it's her appendix."

"Heavens, Nurse, you are an alarmist, aren't you? It's probably something she ate. You run along and stay with her. I'll get a thermometer from my office and come and have a look at her."

But it looked as though the nurse might be correct in her diagnosis. Nurse Petch was doubled up with pain and was in great distress.

Alys put the thermometer in the girl's mouth. "Has she been sick?" she asked the other nurse.

"Yes, Sister."

The pulse was rapid, and when Alys looked at the thermometer it registered well over a hundred.

"When did the pain come on, Nurse?" she asked.

"About an hour ago—and it's been getting worse ever since," gasped Nurse Petch. "Oh, Sister, what am I going to do with it?"

"Don't worry, Nurse. I'll get Dr. Kent over. He is your panel doctor, is he?"

The nurse nodded, and asking the other girl to stay with her, Alys went to her office and rang Richard.

"Ah, the reverend Home Sister," he said as soon as he knew who was speaking.

"This is no time for joking, Dr. Kent," she told him coolly. "One of the nurses is extremely ill. She's in terrible pain. It looks very much like an acute appendix."

He was serious at once. "Thanks for telling me. I'll bring Ben Chalmers or one of the other surgeons with me."

While she was waiting for the two men to arrive, Alys rang Matron and told her what was happening.

"I'll get in touch with her parents right away, Sister," said Matron. "Let me know what the verdict is as soon as you possibly can, won't you?"

Richard and Ben both examined the nurse. She was still in great pain and there was the typical rigidity in the right iliac fossa.

"I don't think there's any doubt about it, Nurse," said Ben. "You've got an inflamed appendix here all right. You'll be better with it out. What do you think, Dr. Kent?"

Richard nodded. "Whatever you say. You're the surgeon."

"Nurse?" queried Ben.

"Oh, Doctor—yes, please—take it out. I can't stand it much longer—" gasped Nurse Petch.

"Yes, yes, all right," he assured her quickly. "Sister will give you something and we'll have you in theatre right away. In a very short time it will all be over. I'll have Dr. Kent give you pentothal, so you won't know a thing about it."

Richard touched the girl's cheek with a tenderness which made Alys's heart leap.

"Poor Nurse Petch," he said gently. "Never mind, you'll soon be O.K. And when it's all over I'll see what I can do about a little holiday for you."

Alys gave the nurse an injection of omnopon and scopolamine. Ben himself rang theatre and gave instructions to the theatre Sister, and Richard ordered a stretcher-trolley to be sent to the Home for the nurse. Alys informed Matron of the decision to operate, and by the time the porter arrived with his stretcher-trolley, Nurse Petch was under the influence of the medication. Alys went with her to theatre herself.

Richard gave the intravenous anaesthetic. Fortunately, some hours had passed since the nurse had eaten, and she had also been sick, so that her stomach was empty. The actual skin preparation was done on the operating table.

Greatly to everyone's relief there was no perforation or peritonitis, but there was a great deal of inflammation and the beginnings of an abscess.

"Shows how great a blessing pain really is," Ben commented. "Another twenty-four hours—and who knows?"

After a short while in the recovery ward the nurse was put to bed in one of the private wards attached to women's surgical and started on a course of penicillin. Alys went to visit her the following day, a very different person from the one who had been gasping with pain.

"Is there anything you'd like from your room,

Nurse?" Alys asked her. "I've brought you your tooth-
brush and other toilet things."

Nurse Petch smiled. "Only my handbag, Sister—oh,
and one or two clean nighties. I'm hoping Mr. Chalmers
will let me go back to the Home—transfer me to sick
bay, I mean, quite soon. Could you ask him, Sister? Or
is it up to Dr. Kent?"

"Not really. You're under the surgeon's care at present. And of course, over here at the hospital, you're
handy for him. I expect he'll transfer you in a day or two,
then you'll come under Dr. Kent's supervision again."

"Did I hear my name mentioned?"

Alys swung round to see Richard himself had entered
the small ward.

"Thought I'd just come and see how my nurse was
getting on. Didn't expect to see you here, Sister
Newton," he added.

Alys rose. "Like you, I came to see how my nurse
was getting on. As a matter of fact, she's anxious to be
transferred to the Nurses' Home sick bay as soon as
possible."

"Is she now? I expect Sister spoils you over there,
does she? Gives you cups of tea whenever you want
them and lets you have visitors at all hours."

"No, she does not, Doctor," Alys retorted. "I'll be
off now, Nurse, and I'll send one of the nurses with
your things, if I can't manage it myself. Good morning,
Dr. Kent."

He gave a mocking bow. "Good morning, Sister
Newton. Don't work too hard over there, will you?"

Alys went out, wishing she'd had something handy to
hit him with. They couldn't meet at all, it seemed,
without some barbed exchange.

Though the nurses all had keys to their rooms many
never bothered to lock them at all. The door of Nurse
Petch's room was unlocked, and Alys went in to get the

articles the girl had asked for. But she stopped short in the doorway. Standing before the open wardrobe, Nurse Petch's handbag in her hand, was Nurse Farrel.

"May I ask, Nurse, what you're doing here? And still more to the point, what you're doing with Nurse Petch's handbag?"

The girl's face flushed a dull red. "I—I was just collecting a few things for her, of course. What do you think I was doing?"

Alys eyed her squarely. "I'm asking the questions, Nurse. And I am not in the mood to accept your rudeness this morning. Did Nurse Petch ask you to bring her bag? Are you a friend of hers?"

"She—she asked me to bring it—yes."

"I can easily check up on that, you know, Nurse. Are you sure she asked you?"

Nurse Farrel gave a deep sigh. "All right. So she didn't ask me. I guessed she'd need it, and as it's my day off and I've nothing better to do this morning, I thought I'd go along and see her and take it to her. Nothing wrong with that, is there?"

"No, Nurse. If you're speaking the truth."

"Of course I'm speaking the truth!" declared Nurse Farrel with the usual lack of respect in her tone.

Then she flung the handbag down on the bed and almost knocked Alys down as she strode out of the room. Alys picked up the bag thoughtfully and opened it. There was a wallet with a little money inside and the usual collection of comb, cosmetics, handkerchief and so on. Alys hated to suspect that Nurse Farrel had been in the act of stealing, but it certainly looked like it. She found a couple of nightdresses and a shopping bag to put them in along with the handbag, in the bottom of the wardrobe. When she left the room she locked the door behind her with her own master key.

She certainly had a problem in Nurse Farrel.

CHAPTER THREE

ALYS was looking forward to her date with Ben, yet she couldn't help wishing, as she put on a crisp cotton dress to meet him, that it had been Richard she was seeing. But the thought vanished as she saw Ben waiting for her at the wheel of his car. He was nice. No one could help liking him.

He opened the car door for her. "Hello there. How are you this evening?"

She settled in beside him. "I've been looking forward to seeing you, Ben."

He flashed her a smile as he let go the handbrake and started the car moving.

"You say the nicest things. I've been looking forward to seeing you, too. I've booked a table at the Royal. They serve a pretty fair meal there."

"Heavens, yes!" It was the best restaurant in town. "You're being very extravagant, Ben."

"Nothing but the best is good enough for the best. Besides, I want to make a good impression on you. Then you'll come out with me again, I hope."

It was nice to be flattered and sought after. A pleasant contrast from the way Richard treated her, she thought wistfully.

It was a wonderfully pleasant summer evening, warm and still.

"Wouldn't it be nice to go off for the day sometime while the weather is like this?" Ben asked. "It seems ages since I was in the country. Nothing is the same when you're alone. And I'm afraid I have been alone since—well, you know how it is."

"Yes, I know."

It was being in love which made everything so much more enjoyable, which put magic into a summer evening and gave the song of the birds an extra thrill. She and Ben couldn't hope to capture that magic, but it would be pleasant, all the same, to have a day out in the country with him. He was such a restful person to be with.

The restaurant, with its décor of pale blue and white, was cool and airy, its waiters unhurried but efficient, and its food delicious. An orchestra played softly and now and then a husky-voiced singer entertained them. This was hardly the place in which to dine alone.

They smiled at each other across the table, as if both were thinking the same thing. But inevitably, they talked shop every now and then.

"I'm sending that nurse of yours back to you tomorrow," Ben said. "She's done very well, and naturally she's anxious to be transferred to the Home. I expect it's more homely over there—if you'll pardon the pun. And, of course, it won't do her any harm to have plenty of visitors."

His mention of Nurse Petch brought the incident of the handbag to her mind.

"You look worried, Alys," Ben observed. "Is anything wrong? You did ask me to transfer her as soon as possible, didn't you?"

"Of course. It's not that. I was thinking of something else. Being Home Sister isn't all beer and skittles, as they say. Or at least, as some people seem to think."

"I'm sure it isn't," he assured her. "And anyone who does think so isn't right in the head. But what's the trouble? Can't you tell me about it?"

So without mentioning Edna Farrel's name, she told him how she had discovered the girl in Nurse Petch's room.

"And had Nurse Petch asked her to take her hand-bag over to her?"

Alys shook her head. "She hadn't asked anyone—except myself."

"And you think this nurse was in the act of robbing Nurse Petch?"

Alys's worried expression deepened. "I really don't know what to think. It certainly looked very suspicious, and she wasn't speaking the truth when she said Nurse Petch had asked her to take the handbag to her. It was only when I told her I could check up on it that she denied it—corrected herself. Anyway, the contents of the handbag were all right. I asked Nurse Petch to look and make sure. The trouble is, this nurse isn't a parti-cularly nice type. She's rude and overbearing. But that doesn't make her a thief—or a potential thief, does it?"

Ben gave her a thoughtful look. "No, but her be-haviour is very suspicious. The thing is, you don't *want* to believe she might be a thief, do you? That's your difficulty. You're too nice a person, Alys. You know that?"

She shook her head. "She's a girl with a chip on her shoulder. Because she's off duty when she's in the Home, she thinks she needn't even call me Sister, still less bow to my authority. It would be awfully tempting to think the worst of her."

He smiled gently. "Then what are you going to do about her? Obviously the business is worrying you."

"I feel a lot better after talking it over. There's noth-ing much I can do, really. I can't report the incident to Matron. That would be much too official—and not fair on the girl if she's innocent."

"You know," Ben said softly, "the world would be a much better place in which to live if everyone were as fair and just as you are. I'd say you're the right person in the right job there. Dealing with fit people can be much more tricky than dealing with the sick. In a way, that girl is right in expecting to get away from the authority of a nursing Sister when she's off duty."

"Richard thinks mine isn't a job for a trained nurse at all."

"Richard?"

"Dr. Kent. He thinks it's a fearful waste of a nurse's training."

"I suppose in a way he's right. Perhaps a different kind of training is required. It certainly isn't a job for just anybody. But of course, we all have to bow to somebody's authority wherever we are."

"I know. I've tried to explain that to her."

"What is she like on the wards?"

"All right. That's the odd thing. She's perfectly polite and correct. Of course, at present, she's on Sister Hurst's ward. And you know Sister Hurst—one of the old school, a stickler for etiquette. I imagine some of the younger Sisters would find her a shade too correct and not natural enough."

Ben tried to change the subject. "We ought not to be talking about work, ought we? Talking shop is like a disease."

"I suppose it is. But it helps sometimes. You know, it's a funny thing about different age groups. At least, up to the age of about thirty. Then age doesn't seem to matter so much. Take me. I'm still fairly young. At any rate, I'm nowhere near middle-aged. But to teen-age student nurses I expect I seem ready for my old-age pension. I suppose they, on the other hand, consider themselves responsible adults, which in some cases they are. Yet to me they appear as young people who need taking care of."

Ben laughed. "Yes, I know what you mean. Of course it's not so much a question of differences in age as in character. Some young people have a sense of responsibility. That's the thing that counts. On the other hand a person can be guilty of irresponsibility at any age. I think that's where our society, in general, is so mistaken in its thinking. This dividing people into age groups is so wrong. Age doesn't really matter all that much. It's character. I've seen teenagers with far more sense, far more able to take care of themselves—and of others —than a good many so-called adults. I'm sure you have yourself."

Alys agreed with him readily. "Some of my youngest student nurses straight out of the P.T.S. are much more responsible human beings than many third-year nurses —or even staff nurses."

"Exactly. For some girls, twenty-one is much too young for them to be State Registered Nurses with all the responsibility that entails. Others State Registration fits like a glove."

"You're quite an observer of life, aren't you, Ben?"

"Am I?" He eyed her with a slight smile. "I did notice that you called Kent by his first name. Do you know him well?"

She grimaced. "Hardly. We always rub each other up the wrong way. He and Olivia seem to hit it off all right."

"Yes."

Ben lapsed into silence for a little while, and Alys wondered whether he was thinking of Olivia.

"Have you ever been engaged, Alys?" he asked presently.

She shook her head. "Not really. At the age of sixteen I vowed eternal love for another sixteen-year-old. At seventeen I almost eloped. At the age of eighteen I started my training."

"And promptly became disillusioned?" laughed Ben.

"Not quite. For the first year I was entirely dedicated

to my new profession—and too tired to do very much except sleep. The second year I began to see a little daylight and went out with a few junior registrars. My third year flashed by so quickly I hardly noticed it. Taking my midder in my fourth nearly brought me to my knees."

"I can well understand that."

She smiled ruefully. "It *was* pretty hectic."

"But you're all right now. You know, I can't think why I never dated you myself. Before I ever knew Olivia, I mean."

"Maybe because you were dedicated, too. St. Anne's is a big hospital. We never got to know each other."

"That was a mistake. But as I remember you used to keep disappearing. One minute you'd be in theatre, the next—a medical ward or night duty."

It was easy, after-dinner conversation, indicative of the fact that he regretted not having known her properly before, and wanted to see her again. Yet she wondered. Weren't they both, at heart, longing to be with someone else? He with Olivia, she with Richard?

Though they lingered pleasantly over their meal, there was still some daylight when they left the restaurant, so Ben drove to a large park a little way out of the town and they walked by the side of a lake there.

"I can't tell you when I had such a nice leisurely evening—or one I've enjoyed so much," Ben told her.

"Me, too, Ben," she said truthfully. She smiled and gave him her hand, ashamed that she had had even the faintest desire to be with someone else—even Richard.

Readily, his hand closed over hers, and she found the touch of it firm and strong.

"What about this next day off of yours?" he asked. "Let's make it a date now, shall we?"

"Next weekend," she told him. "So take your choice. Saturday or Sunday."

"It will have to be Sunday so far as I'm concerned, though I wish it could be both."

"Right. Sunday, then. I may be flat-hunting on the Saturday."

"Really? That will be nice for you—to live out, I mean. You've got more freedom than we have there. We're resident, and resident we have to stay until we rise to be consultants."

It was almost eleven o'clock when they said good-night. But as Alys took the path along the side of the Nurses' Home, she noticed there were quite a number of lights on—some on the junior students' corridor. From one, she heard the sound of a record player. It was very loud. Surely the noise would disturb some of the other nurses?

What she had said to Matron about letting the nurses deal with each other in their own way with regard to the playing of records in rooms was true enough. Usually, it wasn't necessary for her to interfere. But most of the nurses were sensible and didn't play as late as this.

She walked along the corridor from where the music was coming, and was rather dismayed, though not really surprised, to find that Nurse Farrel was the culprit. Alys hesitated. Every time she came into contact with this nurse it was to remonstrate with her about something, which was a pity. She would have liked to get to know her on a more friendly basis. But it was no use being squeamish or making an exception of the girl.

She knocked on the door, and when the voice inside the room called to her to come in, she opened it. Nurse Farrel was alone, propped up in bed, the record player on a chair beside it. She was playing one of the latest pop records, which was not a particularly good one.

Alys smiled at the girl. "I'm sorry, Nurse, but I'm afraid I must ask you to stop playing that now. It's very late and you may be keeping some of the other nurses awake."

Edna Farrel grimaced and turned down the volume. "If it's keeping anyone awake, surely they've got tongues in their heads?"

Alys sat down on the edge of the bed and smiled again. "Maybe. But some don't like to feel they're being mean. If you want to play late it's best to go somewhere away from the bedrooms. The recreation room, for instance, or even the sitting room. Are you on duty tomorrow, Nurse, or is it your day off?"

The girl looked at her in surprise. "Why do you want to know?"

"Because if you are, I'm sure you need the sleep. Do you like that record? Is it one of your favourites?"

Nurse Farrel shook her head, and to Alys's relief and surprise she stopped the record player.

"No, not really. As a matter of fact I've been out. Somebody gave me the record and I thought I'd just try it."

Alys felt quite thrilled at this concession of friendliness. She rose to her feet.

"I'll let you get to sleep, then. Goodnight, Nurse."

"Goodnight, Sister."

Alys could scarcely believe it. For the first time the girl had actually shown a degree of ordinary courtesy, had addressed her as "Sister." Perhaps she wasn't so bad, after all. Perhaps all she needed was a little friendliness, the right approach.

But the very next day two nurses reported missing items of clothing. One had left a pair of pyjamas in the laundry room and when she had returned half an hour later, they had vanished. Another had had a raincoat taken from her wardrobe.

Alys remonstrated with the latter girl for not locking her door.

"I know many of you nurses leave your doors unlocked, but you really shouldn't."

"We don't expect things to be stolen, Sister."

"It's not a very nice thought, I know, but who can tell what prompts people to do these things among such a large number living in the same building? Are you sure you haven't left it somewhere, Nurse? At home or on a bus or something?"

"I'm quite sure, Sister. It was a new one. I've only worn it about twice."

It was very worrying, and something which would just have to be reported to Matron. Alys tried hard to dismiss the picture which came into her mind—the picture of Nurse Farrel, Nurse Petch's handbag in her hands. She didn't want to believe the nurse guilty, especially in view of the change in her attitude last night. At the same time, she mustn't allow herself to be bamboozled just because the girl had called her Sister and decided, for once, to do as she was told.

"Nurse, had your raincoat anything to distinguish it from dozens of others? Any manufacturer's name—or even your own name stamped on it?"

The nurse shook her head. "It hadn't got my name on it. Who does stamp their name all over everything? I bought it from a shop in the town, so I suppose it had some maker's name on it." She went on to describe the coat more fully, colour, size, material and so on.

"All right, Nurse, I'll see what can be done about it. In the meantime, try not to talk about it too much. It may turn up."

Alys searched everywhere she could think of, not really holding out much hope of finding it, since the nurse had been so emphatic about not having left it anywhere. Reading room, library, writing room, cloakrooms, all revealed nothing. Reluctantly, Alys went to see Matron to report the matter. Sister Halesworth, the fairly new Night Superintendent, was just leaving the office, and Alys wondered if she could throw any light on the business. She—or one of her colleagues—usually did a midnight round of the Home, putting out lights and making sure all was well.

But for the moment, Alys merely exchanged a good morning with Sister Halesworth before entering the office at Matron's invitation.

Matron was naturally as shocked and worried as Alys. "This is dreadful, Sister. I don't know when anything like this happened. You say you've searched everywhere thoroughly?"

"Yes, Matron. Everywhere—except any of the nurses' rooms, of course."

"Of course, Sister. I'm afraid there would be quite an uproar if we did that. Is there anyone among the nurses, do you think, who would be capable of helping themselves to other people's property? Strictly between ourselves, naturally."

Alys hesitated. Would it really be fair to mention Nurse Farrel's name? Somehow, she couldn't bring herself to do so. She shook her head.

"I—wouldn't like to say, Matron."

Matron gave her a keen look. "I suppose you wouldn't, but the fact remains that we've got a problem on our hands, and a particularly unpleasant one." She sighed. "I don't want to bring in the police, Sister, if I can help it. I'd rather buy the girl a new raincoat out of my own pocket—and the other one a new pair of pyjamas. But if either of them insist on it, I shall have to. Anyway, Sister, let it lie for a day or two. Both items might turn up. Let us hope so, at any rate. I'll tell Sister Halesworth to keep her eyes open, too."

Later that same day, Alys came across Nurse Farrel ironing a pair of pyjamas which fitted the description of the missing pair. They were white cambric with a pattern of pink rosebuds. Alys felt her heart turn over.

"Are those your pyjamas, Nurse?" she asked.

Nurse Farrel stared at her. "Of course they are. Whose did you think they were? I've no time to be ironing for other people. I've enough to do ironing my own."

Alys felt her patience being sorely tried. "There's no need for you to be rude every time I speak to you, Nurse Farrel. It happens that one of the nurses has lost a pair of pyjamas exactly like those."

The girl's face coloured. She set the iron down with a slam.

"Am I being accused of stealing them?"

Alys drew in a long breath. "You are not being accused of anything, Nurse. It was my duty to ask you if they were yours, and in view of your attitude I had to tell you why I asked. If you want to give people the wrong impression of yourself, you're going the right way about it. If the pyjamas are yours, then there's no more to be said. By the way, do you mind telling me where you bought them?"

"Marks and Spencers."

"Then that explains it. So were the missing ones."

Alys went on her way. Was the girl speaking the truth? But she must be. If she really had stolen another nurse's pyjamas, she would hardly iron them where anyone could see her. Once more, she gave Nurse Farrel the benefit of the doubt. And the following day, both raincoat and pyjamas turned up. The raincoat was hanging in the cloakroom, and the nightwear was found soaking in the second-floor laundry room. Alys checked that they were the missing articles, then telephoned Matron.

"Well, thank goodness for that, Sister. But I must say it's very odd. Unless you were not very thorough in your search, it rather looks as though somebody got scared and decided to replace the things."

"Yes, Matron, it does. The raincoat was definitely not in the cloakroom yesterday. I must admit I didn't make a point of looking in the sinks of the laundry rooms, but the nurse who lost them swears she left them hanging on the rack on the third floor."

"All's well that ends well, anyway, Sister," quoted Matron. "Try to instil it into the nurses to take better care of their things if you can, Sister, without making heavy weather of it."

Was Nurse Farrel responsible? Alys wondered over and over again. As tactfully as she could for the next day or so, she spoke to the nurses about keeping their doors locked. She did not want to make a rule about it, so drawing attention to what could still be regarded as mere carelessness on the part of the two nurses concerned. In any case, the nurses had to hang their personal washing somewhere. Heated chromium rails were in the laundry rooms for that very purpose. Hanging washing in the bedrooms was discouraged, besides there being very little room on the heated towel rails. She hoped earnestly that nothing like this would happen again.

Having to do an evening round of the wards the next time the other deputy Matrons were off duty made a pleasant change for Alys. This consisted mainly of collecting summaries of ward reports, though where there was no Sister on duty she often did a round of the patients, too.

She turned into one of the male medical wards with the realisation that this was one of Richard's wards, and that Olivia Longford was in charge. As it happened, Olivia was on duty. Alys pushed open the half-closed door of the office to see Richard there also.

"Good evening," Alys said, looking from one to the

other. Then, to Richard: "Am I interrupting a consultation? Or are you here to do a round, Dr. Kent?"

Richard's dark brows lifted and a now familiar quirk appeared on his lips.

"Neither, Sister. Sister Longford and I are having a private chat. But I'd hate to think I was interrupting you in the course of your duty. Excuse me—"

He strolled out, both hands in the pockets of his white coat. Alys turned to Olivia.

"Is your report ready, Sister?"

Olivia treated Alys to a barbed look. "Naturally. I must say you're getting very officious these days, Newton. I don't know who you think you are."

"I'm doing my job, that's all." She took the summary report from Olivia and glanced at it. "Not very busy at the moment, are you?"

The medical wards were never quite so hectic in the summer, naturally, as they were in the winter. It was a fair comment, meant to be conversational. But Olivia read criticism into it.

"Busy enough. It annoyed you to find Dr. Kent here for no particular reason, didn't it? I'm sure I don't know how you can stand it over there in the Home. What on earth do you find to do with yourself? Pretty soft job you've got, if you ask me."

Alys ignored her remarks. "Thank you for the report, Sister. If you've nothing to add to it, I'll say good evening to you and let you get on."

"I've *nothing* to add," said Olivia with an almost vicious emphasis.

Alys continued on her way. *Had* it annoyed her to find Richard engaged in a private conversation with Olivia? she asked herself. He hadn't looked as if he were there on official business, even before he had spoken. She supposed that was why she had asked him in the way she had. Normally, in such a situation she would have been discreet and said nothing. But whenever she met Richard she seemed goaded into making some odd remark or other.

On the next ward the Sister was off duty. Alys picked up the report from the desk and went into the ward. The staff nurse was at the medicine cabinet in the centre of the ward checking injections for the senior student nurse to give.

"Everything all right, Nurse?" Alys asked, her experienced eye glancing from one side of the ward to the other. She remembered having this staff nurse as a student when she herself was a ward Sister. The nurse was never very conscientious or efficient.

The staff nurse replied that everything was all right. Alys ran her eye down the report.

"I see you had three admissions today."

"Yes, Sister. A coronary, a diabetic and a nephritis."

"I'll have a word with them, Nurse."

She was appalled to discover that a patient whom she had noticed trying to reach something out of his locker was the very one admitted suffering from coronary thrombosis. Alys made it a rule never to criticise or admonish a nurse in front of a patient if she could possibly help it, especially a staff nurse. It undermined the patient's confidence in those in whom he needed it most. For the moment, she did the next best thing—admonished the patient himself.

"Mr. Hughes, you shouldn't be doing that. Not under any circumstances. If you want anything, call a nurse. And if there are no nurses about you can easily ask an orderly or even one of the up-patients." She smiled to take any edge from her words. "Absolute rest is essential for you for a month or two. We don't want you having another attack such as the one which brought you here."

As it was, the patient was showing signs of dyspnoea.

Alys reached for the man's pulse and found it much more feeble than it should be.

"Give him a few whiffs of oxygen, Nurse, and watch him carefully," she instructed.

"Yes, Sister."

The staff nurse fixed the B.L.B. mask to the man's face, already attached to the oxygen cylinder at the bedside, and saw the grateful look in the patient's eyes as the oxygen began to take effect.

Alys passed on to the second of the day's admissions, the case of acute nephritis, and noticed with satisfaction that the man was being nursed between the new flannelette blankets and was also wearing a soft flannelette bed gown. She looked at his intake and output chart which also appeared satisfactory.

She smiled at the man. "How are you feeling now?"

"Better already, Sister."

She nodded. "Good. Stick to your diet and the amount of fluids ordered by Dr. Kent, and you can't go wrong. Needless to say, you mustn't get up on any account. It's essential that you keep warm."

With regard to the diabetic she was not so pleased. He was looking distinctly drowsy.

"Dr. Kent has seen this patient, of course, Nurse?" she asked.

"Yes, Sister. He's put him on a strict line diet and five units of soluble insulin B.D."

Alys frowned. She spoke to the patient and received no reply. Then swiftly she opened the drawer of his locker, and there was the answer—the outer layer of a bar of chocolate. She beckoned the nurse to follow her into the corridor.

"Get Dr. Kent immediately. No, no, I'll ring him myself. You really must keep a better watch on these patients, Nurse. Remember, they're under *your* care. It isn't enough just to carry out the doctor's instructions. You have to use your observation the whole time."

"But, Sister, how was I to know a diabetic would bring a thing like chocolate in with him? I thought he was asleep."

Alys shook her head. "You can't take anything for granted. Let this be a lesson to you."

She picked up the telephone and asked for Dr. Kent. Within seconds he answered.

"Hello, Sister Newton. Something wrong with one of the nurses?"

"Not this time," she told him. "I'm doing Matron's evening round of the wards and found your new diabetic on Harvey Two gently sliding into a coma."

"What!"

"He had chocolate wrappings in his locker drawer."

"Heavens above! All right. Thanks, Alys. I'll be right over."

She replaced the receiver, absurdly pleased that he had called her Alys. She waited long enough to explain to him that she must continue on her rounds and leave him to Staff Nurse Barnes.

"Oh, must you? Well, thanks for having an eye to my patient. I'm very grateful to you."

He said this without the slightest trace of sarcasm, and she went on her way ridiculously happy.

Alys's weekend off duty started from five o'clock on Friday evening. She strolled out to the little corner shop just outside the hospital and bought an evening paper. She also had a look at the advertisements which were displayed outside, and saw that there was one bed-sitting room to let and two flats. The bed-sitting room gave no telephone number so she decided to ignore that on two accounts. She didn't really want a bed-sitting room and she must be on the telephone in case she were ever needed at the hospital. She returned to the

Home and telephoned the other two and made appointments to see them the following afternoon. Then she looked through the paper. This revealed only one flat, rather a long way out and quite expensive. Still, she might as well go and see it, and she made an appointment to view that, too.

She didn't hold out much hope. She had done this sort of thing for several weekends now and the result was inevitably disappointing. Either the places were badly furnished or unfurnished, and she did not feel she wanted to go to the expense of buying furniture. And yet, she thought suddenly, why not? It would be fun, even if she had to furnish one room at a time. Of course, her father would furnish a place like a shot if she asked him. But as far as possible she liked to be independent. Still, there were some of her mother's things—

CHAPTER FOUR

AFTER lunch the next day Alys went out of the hospital gates and walked towards the bus stop. She hadn't gone far, however, when a pale green car overtook her and pulled up.

"Like a lift?" a voice called out.

It was Richard. She stooped down to speak to him through the open window, a thrill of pleasure coursing through her.

"That depends on where you're going."

He opened the door. "Hop in. I'm not going anywhere in particular."

She did so, and wanted to tease him into one of their battles of wit.

"That's ridiculous," she said, slamming the door after her. "You must have set out to go somewhere."

His lips curved into a smile of amusement. "Well, I could do with a new shirt and a pair of socks. But I can get those any day of the week. Are you going shopping?"

She shook her head. "I'm going flat-hunting."

"Flat-hunting! Heavens above. Sounds as if you might be thinking of getting married or something. You're not, are you?" he asked, quite an anxious note in his voice.

She laughed a little hysterically. "Why not?"

There was a screech of his brakes as he almost drove across some red traffic lights.

"Well, I'd miss you. Who would I have to sharpen my wits on? And who would look after the dear little budding Florence Nightingales?"

"The next 'reverend Home Sister' perhaps."

"Lord! The next one might be middle-aged or something. By the way, you haven't told me where you want to go yet. I'm not a mind-reader."

She took a sheet of paper out of her handbag. "I've got three addresses here, but if you'll just drop me off at one of them—"

"And what do you do after that? Hike it?"

"Well, I can't very well drag you around, can I?"

"You mean you don't want to."

"I mean nothing of the kind."

"Right. Then I'm coming with you. I daresay I'll be getting married myself one of these days, so it will be good experience seeing these flats of yours. By the way, who's the so-called lucky man? Chalmers?" He shot her a sideways glance.

Her heart seemed to be tying itself in little knots. Was he thinking of marrying Olivia?

"What do you mean—'so-called' lucky man?" she demanded, keeping up the repartee with an effort.

"What did you think I meant?" he asked unrepentantly. "That he'll be lucky if he escapes?"

"Very funny indeed," she retorted. "Well, if you really are set on getting in my hair, I believe it's a left turn here."

"Right." He turned the car into the road and stopped at her direction outside one of a row of Victorian family houses. "Oh, I know these kind of places," said Richard. "The landlady usually lives on the ground floor, and if she's the wrong sort, she can be an infernal nuisance. I think it's a good thing I came with you."

Alys gave an amused smile. "I don't know about that. The said landlady will quite likely take one look at you and slam the door in my face. I think you'd better stay in the car. You might prove to be something of a hindrance."

But he ignored her. "I'm coming with you," he said, and promptly got out of the car.

The landlady of this particular house proved to be a replica of the kind of woman Richard had warned her against. A middle-aged woman with dyed auburn hair, wearing carpet slippers and smoking a cigarette, she talked volubly, and every now and again looked archly at Richard.

"Of course, I've no objection to my tenants having their gentlemen friends to see them, so long as they're out of the house by a reasonable hour. I have my reputation to consider. But then, I'm sure—"

Even before she had seen the flat with its oddments of furniture and hideous wallpaper Alys had decided against it. She caught an enquiring look from Richard and shook her head silently, then with inward amusement heard him say:

"I don't really think it's going to suit, thanks."

"You've got a nerve," she told him laughingly when they were back in the car. "I'm supposed to be viewing the places, not you."

"I'm your legal adviser. Or at any rate, your adviser."

To see the second flat they had to climb three flights of stairs, and when they reached it they discovered it was little more than a bed-sitting room, after all. There was barely room to turn around in the bedroom, and the kitchen consisted of a gas ring on the landing. Water had to be carried from the bathroom below.

"It's very reasonable. I've had several people after it," the landlady told them.

"I'm sure you have," murmured Richard.

They went downstairs again. "I'm sorry—" Alys said sadly to the almost bald landlady at the door.

"Well, where do we go from here?" asked Richard at the wheel once more.

Alys sighed. "It's depressing, isn't it?"

"Either of those places were out of the question, anyhow," he answered decisively. "Where is this other flat you've got on your list?"

"The other side of town."

He was taking command, it seemed. Did he really think she was hunting a place for Ben and herself? If only he would show just a tiny bit of jealousy! But why should he? Obviously, he was in a good humour today and was at a loose end. Otherwise, they just wouldn't be together at all. It was practically an accident.

The other address was in a quiet, dignified residential area and the house a large detached one set well back from the road and flanked with tall cypress and other trees.

"Now this looks more like it," announced Richard.

"Yes, I agree. It's more expensive than the other two—and of course I'd have farther to travel every morning. I could get a cycle, I suppose. Or a scooter."

The door was opened to them by a dark-haired woman in her forties.

"Oh, do come in, Miss Newton," she said when Alys had introduced herself. "My name is Wells. Mrs. Wells."

"Thank you. This is a friend of mine, Dr. Kent."

Mrs. Wells led the way upstairs to the first floor. "Was the flat just for yourself, Miss Newton? It's a little on the big side for one. At least, you might think it is. It depends, of course, whether you intend to do much entertaining."

The flat took up the whole of the first floor. A wide landing made the hall on which was a red carpet and some white wrought-iron furniture which Alys thought most attractive. Off this was a sizeable lounge, two bedrooms, a kitchen and dining room and bathroom, all tastefully furnished. Alys went from room to room, lik-

ing it all immensely. She could afford it—just. It would make tremendous inroads into her salary, but with her living-out allowance it wouldn't be so bad.

"If you like—" ventured Mrs. Wells, "I'll leave you to discuss it with your friend for a few minutes while I make some tea. Will you stay and have a cup with me?"

"That's very kind of you." When the door of the lounge had closed behind her prospective landlady, she said to Richard : "Well? What do you think of it?"

He thrust both hands in his jacket pockets. "It's fine. First-rate. An ideal place for a young married couple— or indeed for any married couple. I envy you. Are you going to take it?"

"I think so. A spare bedroom is always handy," she said absently. Why did he envy her? Did he wish he had seen it first? If only he wouldn't keep on harping about marriage. It wasn't really too big for one. She had been used to a large house with plenty of space. After the commodious rooms at home it had taken her quite a time to become accustomed to the small rooms in the Nurses' Home.

Richard was gazing thoughtfully out of the window of the lounge. He turned and looked at her for a moment before allowing his gaze to wander around the room.

"This is definitely your flat," he said in an oddly constrained voice. "In fact, you look quite at home in this room already."

It was beautifully furnished throughout. Alys had a feeling for the place even now. Mrs. Wells had very good taste, and obviously at one time had had the money to indulge it, however she might be placed financially now. A large, good quality Indian carpet covered the lounge floor, the walls were panelled in a décor of ice-blue and white, and on each wall were twin light fittings. There was also a standard lamp, and over the mantelpiece a particularly fine gilt framed mirror. The bedrooms were simply furnished, having none of the cluttered look which Alys hated, and the dining room could equally well be used as a sitting room. It really was more suitable for two people. Perhaps later she could find one of the other Sisters or even one of the staff nurses to share it with her.

Mrs. Wells knocked on the door then and asked if they would care to come downstairs and have tea.

"What do you think of the flat?" she asked as she poured and handed out tea.

Alys assured her that she liked it very much indeed. "I'd love to have it, if you think I'd make a suitable tenant."

Mrs. Wells smiled. "I don't think there's any doubt about that. You don't think it's too big for you, then? Or perhaps you have someone in mind who'll share with you?"

"Well, perhaps, later on, but I promise I'll let you know, if I do, Mrs. Wells."

"It's entirely up to you, my dear. Just feel free to do whatever you wish. Just because I'm the landlady—funny word that, isn't it—and I live in the same building, that doesn't mean you can't do as you like. I just know you wouldn't do anything of which I wouldn't approve, otherwise I wouldn't be letting it to you. I'll give you a key to the front door of the house and you can come and go as you please. Actually, you and I will be the only two people in the house. I'm a widow, you see, and my only son is at university."

At this, Alys offered a little information about herself, liking the woman more and more as they talked. Before she and Richard left, Mrs. Wells had given her the key to the flat and all arrangements had been made for her to move in.

"A very nice woman," Richard commented as they settled in the car again. "You were lucky to find that place. Where now?"

Alys glanced at his profile with amused tenderness. How wonderful it would be if Richard and she were going to live in that flat. She loved him so much. He glanced at her, waiting for her to answer.

"Well, I really haven't anything in particular I want to do now," she told him.

"What, no date tonight with Ben Chalmers?" he asked.

She smiled and shook her head. "He's on duty."

"Oh. In that case, you might as well come into town with me. Come and help me choose some shirts. Then if you're sure Chalmers won't challenge me to a duel maybe we can have dinner together."

She couldn't help laughing at the way he ordered her about.

"All right—if you're sure Olivia won't want to scratch my eyes out," she retaliated.

He let in the clutch and released the handbrake. "Olivia is on duty, too, as it happens, so we're both on the loose as it were, eh?"

In town, he parked the car and then took her arm as they threaded a way through crowds of weekend shoppers.

"So this is what the world and his wife do on Saturday afternoons?" he muttered as they arrived at last at the outfitters where he usually bought his shirts.

It gave her a particular thrill to be shopping with him like this. They looked around the men's department of a large store, and he asked her opinion as to the style and wearing qualities of the various kinds of shirts on display. She was well able to give her opinion, also to say which particular brands she thought were the most reliable and the best buys.

"You seem to know an awful lot about men's shirts," he observed drily. "Who's the man in your life? That is, besides Chalmers and—er—myself?"

She flashed him a glance, absurd little champagne bubbles of happiness sparkling in her eyes that he considered himself one of the men in her life.

"My father, actually," she told him. "My mother died when I was thirteen, so on and off I had the job of shopping for him. Er—who usually helps to choose your shirts and things?"

"My mother—when I'm at home. But that's less and less these days. Home is so far away—the other side of the country, and not very easy to get at. But about these shirts—"

After shirts, he bought socks, then they had a look around the rest of the store, wandering in and out of the various departments. At last Richard announced that his feet were killing him, and Alys that she was dying for a cup of tea.

"I believe there's a café on the top floor. Let's go there before we pass out," said Richard.

The café was by way of the furniture department. As they passed through Alys lingered to comment on some of the attractive contemporary furniture. Richard took her firmly by the arm.

"Come on. We can look at that when we've had our tea. You women! You seem to find it impossible to go from A to B in a straight line."

"Oh, do we? Well, let me tell you, at least we keep our eyes open."

"Don't tempt me to retaliate to that one," he retorted, leading her to an empty table.

It was a wonderfully happy afternoon for Alys. After tea, they wandered around the furniture, admiring both the contemporary and reproduction.

"Wouldn't you have preferred to furnish your flat yourself?" asked Richard.

"In a way. But I quite like Mrs. Wells's taste. I shall leave it as it is for the time being, at any rate. She may not agree to my introducing my own furniture."

"Hm. I should have thought a house would be better than a flat if you're thinking of getting married. For myself, I'd want a house and garden—all complete."

Alys agreed with him. That was exactly what she would want, too. But she made no reply. For a little while she was plunged into despondency. It was dreadful to be in love with a man who could talk in such casual terms about marriage. He lapsed into silence after this, too, and almost without realising it, they found they were outside the store. Alys stood hesitant for a moment.

"Where now?" she asked. "Back to the hospital?"

"Do you want to go back to change, or are you trying to back out of having dinner with me?"

She laughed. "Just giving you a chance to opt out."

He took her arm in a masterful fashion and led her back to the car.

"We'll make a night of it. We'll both change, and in the meantime I'll do some telephoning and book a table somewhere special."

He drove back to the hospital, and with the injunction: "I'll give you one hour flat," he opened the door for her, then they separated.

Her step light, Alys made her way to her room and had a quick bath, then opened her wardrobe, her eyes ranging over its contents. She just hadn't anything to wear. Nothing seemed good enough, special enough, for an evening out with Richard. She really would have to get some new clothes.

In the end she chose a cotton sateen sheath dress in

the newest bold pattern and wore a black edge-to-edge evening coat, with long white gloves, black bag and shoes.

"Very nice," he commented briefly when she joined him a few minutes after the hour.

"Thanks. You don't look so bad yourself. Hope you've managed to book somewhere worthy of all this dressing up."

He had changed into a dinner jacket and looked so handsome it was more than she could bear.

He grinned. "The best there is in the district. Can't do better than that, surely?"

So they dined and danced at the most exclusive hotel in town. Richard was an absolutely wonderful companion. How she envied Olivia his company and the frequent regularity of it she apparently enjoyed. But most of the evening she forgot the existence of Olivia.

At somewhere in the region of twelve-thirty Richard brought his car to a stop in the hospital car park.

"Well," he said, switching off the engine and lights and half turning towards her, "here you are, and I hope you've enjoyed the evening one half as much as I have." He put one hand on her shoulder.

She sighed. "Yes, indeed I have, Richard. It's been great fun."

He drew her towards him then and smiled into her eyes. "I don't know when I've enjoyed a woman's company so much," he said in a low voice.

She knew he was going to kiss her minutes before he did so. She steeled herself in a sort of agony of joy, and when his lips touched hers it was as though the end of the world had come. She closed her eyes, wanting the moment to last for ever. She felt his hands tighten on her shoulders and the pressure of his lips increase, then slowly, he let her go. He gave her a long look and she felt her whole being tighten up, waiting for him to say

something. But the moment passed. He gave a slight smile.

"Yes, it's been fun. Maybe we'll do it again some time."

He squared in his seat, then opened the door and got out of the car and went round the other side to help her out.

"Thanks, Richard," she said, trying to sound normal, though she felt as bleak and hollow as a deserted quarry on a lost world.

She lingered while he locked his doors, then they said goodnight and separated. Alys had never felt herself in such a state of mingled pain and happiness. Oh, Richard, Richard, what am I going to do? her heart cried as she walked the short distance to the Nurses' Home. The evening—the afternoon—the whole day had been wonderful, but—but if only he loved her as she loved him.

As she approached the Home she saw one or two lights she knew to be in bathrooms and landings go out, and guessed that one of the night Sisters was doing her rounds. She would ask whichever of them it was to share a cup of tea with her. She must stop thinking about Richard, somehow.

The night Sister appeared to be on the middle floor. Alys mounted the stairs to try to locate her, and walked along the centre corridor, she popped her head into the wash-place where there were several washbasins and three bathrooms. Sister Halesworth, the Night Superintendent, was just leaving, and Alys's gaze became riveted to the pair of black duty stockings she carried in her hand. She stopped short at the sight of Alys.

"Oh! Oh, Sister, you gave me quite a start." She looked down at the stockings. "Just look at these. How many times do these nurses need telling that there's a laundry room for this sort of thing? I—was just going to take them along there. If whoever it is has left them here has to chase after them, it will teach her a lesson."

Alys looked at her in momentary bewilderment and disbelief, then gave herself an inward shake.

"The nurses often wash out their stockings when they have their bath last thing at night ready for the next morning, Sister. As long as they're not hanging there all next day, I don't really mind. Give them to me, I'll just put them back, otherwise their owner might be late on duty in the morning looking for them. You know what nurses are. They get themselves down to one pair—" As she spoke Alys gently took the stockings from the other's hands and hung them over one of the heated rails. "As a matter of fact, I was looking for you, Sister. I wondered if you'd like to come and have a cup of tea with me when you've finished putting out lights? It won't take a minute to make if you can spare as long to drink it."

"Thanks."

A small, thin, rather wizened little figure with straight brown hair, Sister Halesworth stood still for a moment in the corridor as if lost.

"Come down to my sitting room, then, will you, Sister?" Alys prompted.

Sister Halesworth nodded and continued along the corridor. Alys went down to the first floor to her sitting room a little puzzled. What an odd thing for the Sister to do. As if a pair of stockings hanging in the washroom during the night mattered to anyone. She had done the same thing herself heaps of times. It was nothing to see a whole row of duty stockings hanging up there to dry during the night ready for the following morning. At least, it was until Sister Halesworth came. In fact, what the nurses did quite often was team up their odd mufti stockings and dye them, hanging them in the wash-place to dry.

She plugged in her electric kettle, and it was just on the boil when the night Sister tapped on the door and came in. Alys invited her to sit down.

"The hospital fairly quiet tonight, Sister?" she asked conversationally.

"Fairly. I must say you keep late hours, Newton. I don't know how you do it."

Alys made the tea. "I don't normally keep such late hours. Only now and then. It's my weekend. I don't have to be on duty tomorrow."

"Don't you ever go home?"

"Of course. Sugar, Sister?"

"No, thanks. What pretty cups and saucers," she commented as she took her tea from Alys.

The china was delicate and unusual, and many people remarked on it, but Sister Halesworth seemed particularly intrigued. She fingered the raised pattern of cherry blossom the kimono-clad Japanese figure was tending.

"My father travels a great deal," Alys told her. "He brought this tea-set back from the Far East one time. Both the milk jug and the sugar basin have lids, as you can see."

"Yes, indeed. Lovely."

"And where is your home, Sister?" Alys asked her.

Slowly, the other brought her gaze from the china. "My home? I have none. At least, none to speak of. I was brought up by a foster-mother. She was good, of course, but—" She broke off, gazing into the bottom of her cup.

Alys waited for her to continue, but the Sister seemed lost in thought.

"Had your foster-mother any children of her own?" Alys asked after a minute or two.

"No. The house was full of foster-children," Sister Halesworth answered in an expressionless voice. She drank up her tea, and with another look of appraisal at the fragile china, rose to her feet. "That was a good cup of tea, Newton, thanks. I must be going now."

Alys said goodnight to her and poured out another cup of tea for herself, her mind dwelling on the other woman. She had meant to have a word with her about the recent missing articles of clothing, just to remark on the incidents and ask her if she'd seen anyone acting suspiciously. A little discussion. Yet somehow she had the feeling that it would not have been right. It was odd her removing those stockings. She had begun to roll them up as though—but it was ridiculous. She must have been speaking the truth when she had said she was just going to move them to the laundry room.

Alys rose. What on earth was making her think along these lines? She must be mad. Time she went to bed. She was seeing Ben tomorrow at ten-thirty, and the last thing she wanted was to be droopy.

But she lay tossing for quite some time before she finally drifted off to sleep. Thoughts of Sister Halesworth nagged her. She was an unhappy woman influenced by what was for her, the wrong kind of childhood. Had she no real family, no true friends at all? Somehow, Alys felt extraordinarily worried about her. She could almost feel a concentrated little knot which was tightening somewhere in the middle of her forehead in the shape of the little brown figure of the night Sister.

And yet she was aware of the presence of Richard all about her, his hand on her arm, her shoulder, clasping her hand. There was a smile on his face, half mocking, half tender, and his kiss was on her lips. Small wonder that she dreamed she was searching endlessly along the corridors of the Home for her own room unable to find it. Each room door she opened, thinking that at last she had found it, was occupied by someone else. Olivia,

Sister Halesworth, Nurse Farrel, Olivia again, and again until she was so lost and confused she simply did not know which way to go next. Then at last someone took her by the hand, someone she loved. But she couldn't see who it was, and the next moment the Nurses' Home was full of small children and she was their foster-mother.

She felt far from refreshed when she awoke in the morning, but a maid brought her breakfast, and after several cups of tea and something to eat, she felt better. She had a bath and put on a cotton dress, then slipped a light summer cardigan over her shoulders and went to meet Ben. As she was leaving the Home she almost ran full tilt into Olivia, who gave her a decidedly baleful look. Yet, surprisingly, she stopped.

"Off out for the day, Newton? I saw Mr. Chalmers giving his car a polish quite early this morning."

Alys laughed. "He needn't have bothered on my account. We're only going for a run into the country—and who knows? It might turn to rain."

It did not occur to her until afterwards that Olivia had been merely fishing for the information—or confirmation—as to whether Ben and she were going out together that morning. And unwittingly, Alys had given it to her.

Alys discovered that Ben was very keen on motoring. He did not mind in the least how many miles he drove in order to see a particularly interesting place or beautiful piece of scenery.

"Do you drive, Alys?" he asked her.

"Oh yes. I drove my father's car as soon as I was old enough."

"Never had one of your own?"

"Not on my nursing salary. Father would have bought me one, but I like to be independent—as independent as I can without hurting his feelings. I might have to get one of some kind, though, now that I've got my flat. I was thinking of a scooter."

"A scooter! Oh no, Alys, I wouldn't, if I were you. They're all right in fine weather—and for short journeys, I suppose. But on the whole they're dangerous things. Their small wheels haven't sufficient grip on the road, the rider has absolutely no protection in an accident except from his crash helmet, and of course, that's no use when it comes to a side-on collision."

They approached a road junction where a lorry was parked, blocking the view of anyone emerging from the side road. A car shot out, causing Ben to brake hard.

"See what I mean?" he said. "The fellow couldn't see me, still less a scooter." Then he went on: "You don't need to buy a brand new car, you know. You can get some perfectly good second-hand ones. If you do decide to buy one, let me know, and I'll help you choose one, if you like."

They stopped for lunch at a hotel, and had their coffee on a veranda overlooking some beautiful rose gardens.

"Aren't they gorgeous?" breathed Alys. "They're my father's favourite flower. They were my mother's, too. And I think they're mine."

"You take an interest in gardens?"

"Yes, I love them. I think if I ever marry I'll be quite a keen gardener."

Ben smiled. "What do you mean—*if* you ever marry? If you don't, it won't be for lack of offers."

"We'll let that pass, Ben," she said, laughing.

But she was seized with a sudden longing for just that. A happy marriage, her own garden in which to potter about and grow things. Roses, carnations, lupins, all her favourite flowers.

"If you really want to make a day of it," Ben said, "there are some really wonderful gardens and nurseries at Chester. It's quite a long run, though, and we might be late getting back."

Alys told him she didn't mind that in the least, so long as he didn't.

"It's you who'll be doing the driving, Ben," she reminded him.

"Think nothing of it," he assured her. "If you'd like to go, then let's go. There's some lovely scenery on the way. We can stop off for tea somewhere near Macclesfield."

"It all sounds absolutely gorgeous."

And it was. Ben was a wonderful driver. No wonder he could drive for such long hours without fatigue. He drove at a steady pace, never taking risks or cutting in, and the scenery over the Pennines was breathtaking. They stopped for tea at a place high up where the valley plunged steeply to the silver ribbon of a river and where cattle grazed in the sleepy afternoon. It was so tempting they left the car at the top and took the winding path downwards, hand in hand, and strolled by the riverside for a while, then climbed breathlessly up again, the sun warm on their backs.

It was evening by the time they reached the gardens, but the scent of the roses there came sweetly on the evening air, and Alys wouldn't have missed the visit for the world. They wandered in and out of the various conservatories, admired the magnificent display of dahlias of all varieties. But it was on the way home again that Alys began to feel the effect both of the long drive and her disturbed sleep of the night before.

"Ben, I don't know how you can keep it up," she said, after she discovered her head rolling from side to side, as she almost fell asleep.

He glanced sideways at her and smiled. "Tired? Lean your head on my shoulder and have a sleep. I'll wake you up when we get there."

She did so, and was soon lulled to sleep by the gentle movement of the car. But suddenly she was jerked wide awake as Ben applied his brake sharply. At the same time there was the sound of breaking glass and an ominous crash of metal meeting metal in an unmistakable collision.

CHAPTER FIVE

"BEN! What on earth has happened?"

"Sorry if I scared you, Alys. The car in front—overtook me and collided with another one doing the same thing coming the other way. I'd better go and see if there's anything I can do."

It was quite dark now. Already there was a long line of cars on either side of the road like strings of glow worms in the blackness of the night.

"I'll come with you," Alys said. "Do you think it's a real head-on collision?"

"Probably their offside lights and wings. I wonder why the idiots do it? By the way, there's a beacon light in the boot, Alys. Would you get it out? We may need it. You'll find a first aid kit there, too. I always carry one with me in case of an emergency like this."

It was as Ben had predicted. The wings of both cars were locked together, their offside lights smashed. Alys handed Ben the beacon light, then went to see if there was anyone injured. In both, she found a woman passenger badly bruised and shaken. She gave what comfort and treatment she could, while the drivers and Ben, assisted by two other motorists, struggled to extricate the two cars which were blocking the road.

As one of the motorists not involved remarked, it was a mercy no one was killed. As a surgeon, Ben felt it his duty to emphasise this, and to remonstrate with the two drivers who had caused the accident.

"If you place little value on your own lives, you might at least consider that of your passengers," he told them.

"Overtaking at night is absolutely dangerous unless you have a good clear road in front of you."

"We don't need you to tell us," one of them said in a disgruntled tone.

"It seems you do," retorted Ben. "I just hope this will be a lesson to you, that's all."

Ben made sure that the drivers were not too shaken to carry on and that their cars were undamaged mechanically, and also let the traffic congestion ease up before starting on his own way, by which time he and Alys had been delayed over an hour.

"It's a wonder there wasn't a real pile-up," he said as they continued on their journey. "I started to slow down as soon as the man behind me began to overtake, and I've no doubt that the man behind the other car did the same. I signalled like mad to the man at the back of me with my brake lights."

"I don't suppose those kind of drivers realise that quite often they owe their very lives to good drivers like you," commented Alys. "Do you think they will have learned from the experience?"

"One of them might. The other seemed pretty cocky, and unrepentant. I hate preaching, but I really felt I ought to try to rub it in a bit."

They called at a transport café for a cup of coffee, and did not arrive at the hospital until the small hours of the morning, by which time Alys was so weary she could barely stagger.

"Poor Alys! Let me see you to the Home. I'm terribly sorry about all this. I knew we'd be late, but of course I didn't foresee that we'd be as late as this."

"It's not your fault, Ben. Apart from the accident, it's been a wonderful day, and I've enjoyed it immensely."

He put his arm about her shoulders and walked with her towards the Home.

"Front entrance?" he asked.

She laughed a trifle weakly. "Yes. Fortunately, there isn't likely to be anyone up to see me coming in at this hour, because I simply couldn't make it up the basement steps."

But when they reached the front entrance she was never so surprised in her life. She almost collided with Richard. They exchanged an astonished stare, then Richard looked at Ben.

"Well, well! You certainly have made a day and a half of it, haven't you?" he observed.

Alys stared at him. "Richard, what's happened? What are you doing over here at this hour? Is somebody ill?"

His dark brows raised in mock surprise. "I'm glad you're interested. It's one of your flock. Nurse Farrel. She tripped over her dressing gown—one of those lethal long things—and fell down the stairs."

"Nurse Farrel! Oh, that poor girl. How is she? Was she badly hurt?"

He pursed his lips. "No bones broken, as far as I can make out. But she's a mass of bruises and she knocked her head as she landed at the bottom."

"Was she unconscious?"

He nodded. "Hm-hm. Caused quite a commotion. One of your junior nurses thought she was dead, said she wasn't breathing. Anyway, I've had her put to bed in the sick bay. Night Sister is with her at the moment. You couldn't be found. In any case you were off duty, I suppose. I'll be over to see her in the morning. You know the treatment for head injury, I'm sure, Sister. Goodnight." Then he added, unable to resist the quip, it seemed : "Or rather, good morning!"

As he went off, Alys turned worriedly to Ben. "Poor Nurse Farrel! She always seems to be in trouble, somehow. I must go and have a look at her. Goodnight, Ben —and thanks for the day and everything."

She glanced up at the clock in the entrance hall as she entered the building. It was two-thirty. How long ago had this happened? It must have been during the last half hour or so, as Richard was only just leaving. What was Nurse Farrel doing up at this hour? And why was she on an upper floor? Her own room was on the ground floor.

Alys made her way to the sick bay. Sister Halesworth was just leaving. She looked at Alys in surprise.

"I thought you must be sleeping out, Sister. Have you only just come in?"

Alys nodded. "There was an accident on the road. I stopped to help. How is Nurse Farrel?"

"It's hard to say. She keeps coming and going. Nurse Amos, the nurse who found her, is sitting with her for the moment until I can think who to send over to stay with her. She's on a half-hourly pulse, of course."

"I'll stay with her for a little while, Sister, and send Nurse Amos to bed."

Sister Halesworth shrugged. "As you like. You look as if you could use some sleep yourself, but of course, it's none of my business how late you stay out. I wouldn't have thought it was a very good example to set the nurses. However, I'll send somebody along just as soon as I can."

Alys let her go without answering. What use was it to retort that it was hardly usual to find any nurse up at this hour, in any case, to be an example to, good or bad? Or to make any attempt to defend herself to the other woman. As she had said, it was none of her business.

She went into the sickroom where young Nurse Amos was sitting by Nurse Farrel's bed in the dim light of the shaded bedside lamp. Alys buttoned up her cardigan over her cotton dress.

"It's all right, Nurse Amos. You can go to bed now. I'm sitting with Nurse Farrel for a little while."

Nurse Amos drew her dressing gown around her as she stood up. "Thank you, Sister," she said.

Alys drew her to the door. "What were you doing up at this hour, Nurse? Are you all right yourself?"

The nurse blinked. "I got up to pay a call, Sister, that's all. I heard a noise and a cry and ran to see what was happening. By the time I reached the foot of the stairs Nurse Farrel was just lying there still. She—she wasn't breathing at all, Sister. Honestly, I thought—"

"It's all right, Nurse. It's one of the symptoms. You did well to get Dr. Kent. Off you go to bed now. And unless you're very wide awake when you're called in the morning, stay in bed for an extra hour and go on duty at nine. I'll make it right with your ward Sister."

The nurse thanked her and said goodnight. Alys went back to the bedside. Nurse Farrel was lying with her eyes closed, whether in natural sleep or not it was hard to say. Alys put her fingers on the girl's pulse. She must be watched carefully for any sign of compression. This would mean pressure on the brain from either a blood clot forming between the dura mater and the skull or a depressed bone. At the moment, however, her pulse was quick and rather weak and her skin inclined to be cold and clammy—the usual symptoms of shock. The girl's eyelids flickered and opened.

Alys spoke to her softly. "Hello, Nurse. How are you feeling now? You must have had a very nasty fall."

Nurse Farrel frowned slightly. "Yes, I—I suppose I did. What—time is it, Sister?"

"Getting on for three o'clock in the morning."

The girl winced suddenly. "I ache all over."

"Just aching? No particular pain anywhere? Or headache?"

Nurse Farrel shook her head. Alys reached for the

thermometer on the bedside table. "I'll take your temperature while you're awake. One of the night nurses is coming to stay with you later. You knocked your head, you know, as you fell, so you'll have to stay in bed for a day or so, or even longer. We can't afford to take any chances with a head injury."

Nurse Farrel frowned as if trying to remember something. "I—thought Sister Halesworth was here."

Alys nodded and glanced at the thermometer. The girl's temperature was sub-normal.

"She was. She's gone back over to the hospital."

"Oh." The heavy lids closed again.

Alys watched her for a moment, then rose. Whatever happened she simply must not fall asleep herself. She went into the sick bay kitchen and put on the kettle. A cup of tea would keep her awake for another hour or so, but she hoped Sister Halesworth would not be long in sending a nurse over. When she had made the tea she took it into the sickroom and drank it by the bedside. How severe was the nurse's concussion? she wondered. She appeared to have a little post-traumatic amnesia, but perhaps when she awoke in the morning she would be all right. What had she been up to at that hour in the morning? And why had Sister Halesworth been so late in doing her round of the Home?

Alys took Nurse Farrel's pulse again and found it steadying a little. Shock subsiding or the onset of compression? She hoped it was not the latter.

"Watch her carefully, Nurse," she said to the night nurse whom Sister Halesworth sent over about half an hour later. "Report any sign of cerebral irritation, and if there is any appreciable slowing of the pulse or rise in temperature or irregularity of the respiration rate, notify Night Sister immediately."

"Yes, Sister."

Alys made her way to her room and staggered into

bed, asleep almost before her head touched the pillow. But it seemed to her that no sooner had she dropped off to sleep than she was awakened again by a maid with her breakfast, and she realised it was nine o'clock. She opened her eyes with difficulty and sat up, her first thought for Nurse Farrel. She drank a cup of tea, then ran the comb through her hair and pulled on a house-coat. She would go along and see how the nurse was and have her breakfast afterwards.

She stopped short, however, as she entered the sick-room, and felt her cheeks colouring. Richard was there.

He glanced round. "Hello," he said with a smile of amusement. "Come in, do."

He was accompanied by the second deputy Matron, who said, "Good morning, Sister Newton," as if there was nothing unusual in a Sister appearing before a doctor during his round in her dressing gown.

"I—I just came to see how Nurse Farrel is," she said, half turning to go out again.

"Your anxiety does you credit, Sister," said Richard. "She's not doing too badly at all."

"Oh. Oh, thank you. I'll—come back later."

He flicked her another amused glance before turning back to his patient. Alys felt an upsurge of annoyance. He was always laughing at her, always in the wrong place at the wrong time. Take last night, for instance. Her coming in at that hour with Ben. It couldn't have been better—or worse—timed than if hours had been spent planning it. It just *would* have to be Richard who happened to be leaving the Home at that precise moment.

She was glad to hear Nurse Farrel was a little better, anyhow, she thought as she ate her breakfast. Though she was not officially on duty until one o'clock, she thought she might as well put on her uniform right away. This she did, and was just going to see her patient again when her telephone rang to say there was an outside call for her. It was her father, home again after his latest trip abroad.

"I've just got back, Alys," he said. "At least, late last night. How are you?"

She asked him about his trip, then told him about the acquisition of her flat.

"Oh, then you simply must have a car, my dear," he said—as she guessed he would—as soon as he knew she would have a little distance to travel each day. "Just choose the one you'd like and have the bill sent to me."

"Oh, but, Father—" she began.

She heard his exclamation of impatience. "Now look here, my dear. Are you my daughter or aren't you?"

"But, Father, you know I want to stand on my own feet."

"My dear girl, you've been doing that for the past six years or so. Surely I can give you a little present now and then?"

She smiled to herself as she thought of the expensive fur coat he had bought her at the end of her convalescence—the coat which had brought that certain look from Richard at their first encounter at the railway station.

"I thought of looking around for a second-hand car, Father," she told him. "I can just about manage that with what I have in the bank."

She heard the great sigh he heaved. "Well, if it's a second-hand car you're after, you can have mine. I was about to get a new one, anyway. And if it will please you I'll take what a dealer would give me—and you needn't be in a hurry to pay me. As a matter of fact, I'll bring it down. I was thinking of paying you a visit, anyway. Will you be able to put me up at that flat of yours?"

She said she would, and told him when she was moving in.

"Right. I'll come down next weekend and have a look at you. Expect me somewhere about lunchtime."

"I shall be on duty, Father. Make it the weekend after that," she said. "And, darling, thank you."

"But in the meantime, how are you going to get backwards and forwards to the hospital?" he demanded.

She laughed. "Don't worry, Father. I expect there are buses. Goodbye."

She hung up, a soft, tender smile on her face. He was a dear. He would spoil her utterly if she would let him. She knew quite well that until he knew she needed a car he had had no thought of getting a new one for himself, and she also knew that he would put the price ridiculously low. He could have easily afforded to foot the bill for a new car for her as he had suggested. Indeed, several cars. He was a very prosperous businessman, managing director of a chain of stores well known throughout the country. But there was not one person at the hospital who knew about this.

When she reached the sick bay she found Matron there, but no nurse at the bedside.

"Dr. Kent thought Nurse was out of immediate danger and didn't really need a special. She's now on a two-hourly T.P.R.," Matron told her. Then: "I see you're already in uniform, Sister. Why is that?"

"I thought I might as well, Matron. There might be something I can do for Nurse Farrel." She smiled down at the girl in the bed, now awake, but with a still-sleepy look about her eyes, Alys thought. "It's getting near eleven. Perhaps she'd like a cup of coffee."

"Well, that would be very nice," Matron answered for the girl. "Would you like that, Nurse?"

"Yes, Matron."

"Good," Matron said cheerfully. "Then I'll leave you,

Sister. Don't bother to see me off," she said, bustling away.

Alys looked down at her patient. "Well, how are you, Nurse? Still sore?"

Nurse Farrel nodded. "Every time I move."

"It will pass, though you may not think so at the moment. I'll make that coffee—and you shall have it in my pretty cups. How would you like that?"

An odd sort of frown appeared on the girl's brow. "I—don't know."

Alys looked at her and smiled a little. "I expect you're still feeling woozy, aren't you? Don't worry. Just lie quiet and I'll be back as soon as I can."

The girl did not seem quite right yet, Alys thought as she went to her sitting room to get the Japanese china Sister Halesworth had admired so much. She must have a talk to Richard about her as soon as possible. Perhaps he would be coming over to see her this evening.

She made instant coffee, one for her patient, and one for herself, and took them into the sickroom on a tray with a small tin of biscuits. For some reason Nurse Farrel looked most disturbed. She stared at the two cups of coffee as if afraid Alys was going to poison her.

"Is anything bothering you, Nurse?" she asked.

"No-o. No, I—of course not."

"Come along, then, I'll help you to sit up a little bit." She brought two extra pillows from one of the other beds, and put her arm under the girl's shoulders. "Gently does it. That's right. There, how's that?"

"Thanks."

Alys sweetened the coffee for her and put the cup and saucer into her hands. Still there was that look of perplexity in the girl's eyes, the frown creasing her brow.

"Biscuit?" Alys held out the tin, wondering what was wrong with her.

She shook her head to a biscuit. Alys took one herself then sat down at the bedside with her own coffee.

"Do you remember what happened last night, Nurse?" she asked. "Or rather, this morning."

Nurse Farrel looked at her, startled. "What—do you mean, Sister?" she asked jerkily.

"I mean—do you remember falling?"

"I—I don't know. It's all such a blur." Again, the perplexed frown.

"What were you doing out of bed at that hour?"

"I—I don't know. I heard a noise—I think." The frown on the girl's forehead deepened and she became agitated. Her lips began to tremble and the cup and saucer shook in her hands.

"Never mind," soothed Alys quickly. "Drink your coffee, then lie down again."

It was when she was putting the two cups and saucers in her cupboard again that she discovered there was one of each missing. She checked and re-checked in case she had mis-counted, or the sixth cup and saucer had become hidden or she had put them in the wrong place.

"Oh, no!" she breathed to herself as the horrible truth was forced upon her.

Someone had been into her sitting room and taken them. Why? There was only one answer—unless they were returned quite soon, which was hardly likely. They had been stolen. Alys almost groaned aloud. She would rather have broken the whole set. Who this time? The same person who had stolen the other things—the pyjamas and raincoat?

Feeling sick at heart, Alys sank into a chair. Nurse Farrel had been up during the small hours of the morning. Why? She closed her eyes in despair as she recalled the girl's agitation at the sight of the cups and saucers, and her confusion that might or might not have been due to her head injury.

There was a knock at the door and she called out to the person to enter. It was one of the ward Sisters—and Alys suddenly remembered Nurse Amos whom she had told to sleep in because of her disturbed night.

"Oh, Gregory, I'm so sorry. I forgot to tell you that I told Nurse Amos she could have extra sleep this morning if she felt she needed it."

Sister Gregory nodded. "Yes, I know. She told me. It's all right. It's not that I've come to see you about."

Alys invited her to sit down, an awful feeling in the pit of her stomach. "What is it, then? You look a little upset."

"Well, I am rather. I left a set of underwear in the laundry room last night, and they've vanished. I wouldn't mind so much, but I've only worn them once, and they were rather expensive."

Alys's stomach turned over. "Oh dear, this is awful, Gregory. You've had a good look all around, have you?"

The other nodded. "I've searched for an hour or more. All the bathrooms and the laundry rooms on the other floors, my drawers and everything, just in case—" She broke off, then went on : "I'm afraid this isn't the first time I've missed things. Duty stockings mostly. But I didn't bother to report those. It's so easy for someone to mistake other people's for their own."

Alys felt in despair. She said nothing about her missing cup and saucer. It would only make matters worse. She asked the Sister for a description of the missing underwear and what brand they were.

"I'm terribly sorry about this. I'll report the matter to Matron, of course, and in the meantime I'll keep a look out for them. We don't want to get the police in if we can possibly help it. All the same, I do wish I could find out who is responsible."

Alys said this almost with tongue in cheek. In one

sense she dreaded finding out who was responsible. She hated even suspecting anyone, but too many articles had been missing for there to be any question of their owners misplacing them.

"You know," said Sister Gregory, "I can never remember anything like this happening before, and I've been here eight years. Have you got any idea who it might be?"

Alys had, unfortunately, but she shook her head. "I wouldn't like to say at this stage, anyway. Gregory. You understand?"

"Of course. Well, I'd best be getting along. It's a pretty horrible business, and it would be as well if you *could* find out soon and deal with whoever it is. Otherwise, somebody is going to have something missing who will *demand* that the police be brought in, whether we like it or not."

Alys had to admit the truth of this. *Could* Nurse Farrel be the culprit? All the evidence pointed to her. But uneasily she remembered coming across the night Sister with those black stockings. Of course, it was ridiculous to even think of her as being a person who would indulge in petty theft. With her salary what possible motive could she have? No, it was much more likely to be someone like a junior nurse or cleaner whose salaries were not so large as those of the Sisters and staff nurses.

Alys went back to the sick bay. Nurse Farrel was lying with her eyes closed, but her features were by no means composed in sleep. Alys stood looking down at her for a moment. Was she feigning sleep, and if so, why? After a minute or two Alys went out again. It was all very difficult. She did not want to worry the girl with too many questions at this stage. She should be kept quiet and not excited, until she had recovered a little more, at any rate.

Extremely worried about the whole business of these petty thefts, Alys wandered from one bathroom and laundry room to another in the hope of coming across Sister Gregory's missing underset, but as she feared, it was a fruitless search. About her cup and saucer she tried not to think. She valued the set, naturally, but if only the other items would turn up, she wouldn't mind so much about the china. She could, of course, go into Nurse Farrel's room and see if the missing articles were there. But the idea of searching all the girl's drawers without her permission was repugnant to Alys. She would have to wait until the nurse was a little better, out of danger, then talk to her honestly about the matter.

Matron, too, would have to be told, Alys decided. In any case, there was little point in trying to hide anything from Matron. Alys had known her for many years now, and knew that she was not the kind of woman to take too-hasty action.

"I'm afraid, Sister," Matron said gravely, "that we're not going to be able to let this go on for much longer without doing something about it—getting in the police. It doesn't have to be a man in uniform, you know. In fact, they would almost certainly send a plain-clothes detective. Of course we don't want a lot of talk and gossip about the business. On the other hand, bringing in the law might well throw a scare into whoever is responsible and put an end to the thefts. I did ask Sister Halesworth what Nurse Farrel was doing up at that hour of night, but she couldn't say. It's all very worrying and distressing, Sister," sighed Matron, "and I really will have to take action. However, we'll let it ride for another day or so until Nurse Farrel is better, then she must be tackled about her wanderings in the middle of the night. I agree it would hardly be fair to search her belongings, but I'm afraid that, if and when the police are called in, they will have no such compunction."

When Alys returned to the Home and popped in to see how Nurse Farrel was, she found her bed empty. She looked in the bathroom and toilet, but there was no sign of the nurse in either places. Alys went in search of her, to find her just returning.

"Nurse, where on earth have you been? You had no right to get up at all. Dr. Kent said you were to stay in bed. Who knows what harm you might be doing to yourself," she scolded, then repeated: "Where have you been?"

"To my room. There was something I wanted."

"You should have asked me to get it for you—whatever it was."

She could see nothing in the girl's hand, but not wanting to nag, said no more. She saw her into bed again, wondering what had been the real reason for the nurse going to her room.

In the late afternoon Richard came to see Nurse Farrel, and seemed fairly satisfied with her condition.

"All the same, keep her in bed for another day. We can't afford to take chances." He had a few words with the nurse, then went on, "She doesn't seem very cheerful. In fact, I'd say she's inclined to be depressed. Or is she always like that? You know her better than I do. At least, you should."

Alys frowned a little. "I don't know. She's a difficult girl in many ways. I wouldn't say she's ever very bright and cheerful. At the same time, I think she is a little depressed, though whether it's anything to do with her fall I wouldn't like to give an opinion."

"What makes you say that?"

She hesitated. He had a right to know, she supposed, as the girl's physician. And yet the trouble in the

Nurses' Home was not a thing to be talked about. It had really nothing to do with Richard.

"I'd—rather not say, if you don't mind," she told him. "But there's one thing you should know. She's been up. She went to her room while I was over at the hospital seeing Matron."

"Did she? Well, it doesn't seem to have done her any harm. I'll take your word for it that her depression might have other causes than her fall."

There was something different about his manner. She missed his banter, his wit. She walked with him to the door of the Home and he barely spoke. Her heart was heavy. She would rather have his sarcasm than this.

"Is anything wrong, Richard?" she ventured.

He turned and looked at her, mild surprise showing in his eyes.

"No—why?"

She smiled ruefully. "I'm so much used to your—insults. It seems all wrong, your being so polite—and so quiet."

His dark brows shot up in that characteristic way he had, and a faint smile touched his lips.

"When are you moving into that palatial flat of yours?" he asked. "Let me know, and I'll run you along there. That is, if I'm not treading on Chalmers's corns."

She smiled. This was better. Anything was better than his treating her as if she were just one of the Sisters and nothing more.

"I don't think Ben has got any corns. I'm not really moving in until my next weekend, the one after next. My father is coming down. He's bringing me his old car. I said I was thinking of buying a second-hand one, so he suddenly decided to have a new one."

"Some father," he commented, giving her an odd look. "And how old is the old car?"

She smiled. "Not very, I suspect. I'd—like you to meet Father. He'll be staying the weekend. Perhaps—"

She broke off, realising he wasn't listening to her. She followed his gaze and saw Olivia Longford coming towards them.

"Yes, all right, Alys," he said absently. "I'll be seeing you again before then, anyway."

He made off, and Alys lingered at the door just long enough to see him and Olivia meet and stop to talk. She turned and went indoors. How much did Olivia mean to him?

CHAPTER SIX

A DAY or two later both Alys's cup and saucer and Sister Gregory's underset turned up. Alys discovered her cup and saucer in the cupboard along with the rest of the matching china. She had gone to the cupboard for something else, and had automatically run her eye over the set, half hoping, but not for a moment believing that in some magical way the set was complete. She had hardly been able to credit her own eyes when she counted six cups, then six saucers. How the sixth had got there she had no idea. She just knew they had not been there before. She had counted the set too many times on discovering one of each missing to have been mistaken.

As to Sister Gregory's underset, this was found hanging in the laundry room of the night nurses' corridor.

"It's most extraordinary," said Matron when Alys reported the discovery of the missing items. "All these things disappearing, then turning up somewhere. On the face of it, all the incidents could be put down to carelessness, property misplaced rather than stolen. Or even just mistakes. You're quite sure, for instance, that you counted your tea-set thoroughly?"

"Oh yes, Matron, quite sure," Alys assured her.

"Hm. Well all I can say is, it's a good thing I wasn't too hasty in calling in the police. I wonder if there's any significance in the fact that Sister Gregory's underset turned up in the night nurses's corridor? The night nurses certainly have a good chance of doing anything like this while all the day staff are on duty. And it would

88

almost seem that somebody has got scared of the possibility of our calling in the police."

Alys sighed. "It's very hard to say, Matron. About the night nurses, I mean. I'm always somewhere around during the daytime. I usually know which night nurses are having their nights off, and if I see a night nurse up during the day I find out why—ask her whether she's finding difficulty in sleeping."

It was all very puzzling. As she returned to the Nurses's Home after seeing Matron, Alys remembered how a few mornings ago, Nurse Farrel had been missing from her bed. Had she really been to her room, as she said, or had she been returning the cup and saucer and Sister Gregory's underwear? Alys did not use that china every day. The two pieces could have been returned a day or so ago without her discovering them.

The day before Alys was due for her weekend—the weekend she was expecting her father to visit her, Richard pronounced Nurse Farrel out of danger.

"What about a week's leave, Nurse? You'd like that, I suppose?" he said.

But she surprised him by shaking her head. "I'd sooner go straight back on duty. I've had enough of hanging about, and I feel all right."

Richard shrugged. "As you like. Any other nurse would have jumped at the chance of a bit of sick leave. Why don't you want to go home, eh?"

But Edna Farrel maintained an obstinate silence, and Richard said no more to her.

"Odd sort of lass," he commented to Alys. "She has got a home to go to, I presume?"

"I suppose so. I'm not sure. It's difficult to get her to talk about herself. I thought I was getting somewhere with her once, but this fall of hers seems to have made her more unapproachable than ever."

"Shouldn't think that has anything to do with her

fall directly," Richard said briefly. Then, eyeing her: "Don't look so worried. People are what they are, and you can't do much about it."

Alys did not agree with him, quite, but she did not argue. She really had been making headway with Nurse Farrel. She was sure of it. She gave an inward sigh and dismissed thoughts of the nurse for the moment.

"I'm beginning the great move into my flat tomorrow evening," she told him. "My father is arriving Saturday lunchtime."

Richard gave a swift smile. "Oh yes, I said I'd run you down there, didn't I? Can't make it Friday evening, though. Would Saturday morning—first thing—be all right?"

She told him it would. "I'll have everything packed Friday evening."

"Right, then," he said, and with a parting smile which sent her spirits soaring, he strode off.

Perhaps there was nothing serious between him and Olivia Longford, after all, she thought joyfully. She packed her belongings into her trunk and suitcases as excitedly as though she were going on a trip around the world. Her father would be going back to London on Sunday afternoon. Perhaps Richard would have tea with her at the flat, too, and supper. He must like her a little, otherwise he wouldn't have suggested running her along to the flat in the first place.

She realised afresh how many possessions one could collect in a short time. It was past midnight by the time she had crammed everything into every available box or bag as well as her cabin trunk and large expanding suitcases. Nevertheless, she was awake and up early the following morning, and telephoned a porter to help her to carry it all down to the ground floor. She realised a little ashamedly that she had not even spared a thought for Ben until she answered the telephone to him just as Richard arrived at the door of the Home.

"I've only just remembered that it's your weekend," he said. "What about having dinner with me tonight? Or if you can't manage that, perhaps we could have tea in the country somewhere on Sunday."

"Ben, I'm sorry. Didn't I tell you? My father is coming for the weekend, and—"

She broke off in some confusion, glad that Ben could not see her face. She ought to invite him to meet her father, or at least to tell him she was seeing Richard, but she didn't.

Ben said quickly: "Oh well, if your father is coming, you'll want to be with him, naturally. Some other time, then, Alys?"

"Of course."

She would tell him about Richard's offer to help her move in next time she saw him. She replaced the receiver, then, her heart giving a skip and a jump as she caught sight of Richard's figure in the doorway of the Home. He eyed her various pieces of luggage in the vestibule.

"Good grief, Alys! Is this all yours? The stuff you women accumulate!"

"I'm sorry, Richard. Do you think you're going to get it all in?"

He grinned. "I expect so. The trunk will just about go in the boot, but the lid won't fasten, of course. Still, that won't matter."

He picked up two of the cases with as much ease as though they were empty and thrust them on to the back seat of his car. Alys followed with a couple of smaller ones, then she helped him with the trunk.

"You're quite sure there's nothing else?" he teased her when everything was stacked in.

"You offered your services," she reminded him. "Want to back out?"

"What—and unload again? Hop in, woman, and let's get going."

She loved being chivvied by him. She loved sitting beside him. Indeed, her head was so much in the clouds she quite forgot that she had absolutely no food in the flat. It was Mrs. Wells who reminded her.

"Knowing you were moving in today, I took some extra milk, Miss Newton. But I didn't know quite what to do about bread and so on for you. I'm afraid the tradespeople don't like delivering on Saturdays—"

Alys smiled and thanked her. "That's all right, Mrs. Wells. I'll pop along to the shops myself. We can have a cold lunch, and maybe go out to dinner."

"Fine housekeeper you are," Richard chided Alys as he deposited her luggage in her bedroom. "We'd better get this shopping lark organised. Make a list, and I'll go to some shops while you go to the others, otherwise you're not going to be in time to meet your father. And by the way, are you sure he'll want me around? Don't you think I'd better push off when I've helped you with your shopping?"

Alys thought fleetingly that even if she did not already love him, she would fall in love with him now. She flashed him a smile, thinking her love for him must surely be only too obvious.

"No, I *don't* think you'd better push off. Father would love to meet you, I know. I'm sure you and he will get along together famously. And by the way, I don't have to meet him at the station. Had you forgotten? He's coming by road—in the car I'm supposed to be buying from him."

"Why do you say 'supposed'?".

She laughed. "If I know Father, he'll want to *give* it to me. Or name a ridiculously low price."

Richard gave her an odd look. "He can afford to give a car away and buy a new one—just like that?"

"Well—yes."

She left it at that. Somehow she did not want Richard to know just how rich her father was, or who he was. She had long discovered that, even in the present day that sort of thing made a difference to a relationship. People on whom she thought she could have staked her life had become shy of her, or made up to her falsely, or at best become less than natural as soon as they learned who her father was. This applied to women was well as men. But most of all, of course, to men. Alys had had virtually to fight for her independence, and only her love for her father induced her to accept gifts from him from time to time.

She felt she simply could not bear it, if Richard began to fight shy of her because he did not want to risk being accused of being "after her money." She was her father's only child and heir.

She saw Richard's expressive brows raise slightly, then he shrugged swiftly and reminded her about her shopping list.

"We haven't got much time, anyway. The shops will be crowded, Saturday morning and all that."

Alys could have laughed aloud at the way he was taking charge. Obediently, she found a sheet of paper, and for the next quarter of an hour applied herself to the task of trying to think of every possible requirement for the food cupboard, prompted by Richard, without whose help she doubted whether she would have even thought of such things as pepper and salt, mustard, washing-up powder, or a toilet roll.

Together they went round a supermarket, ending up with twice as many goods as had been on their list. Then Richard went to the butcher's while Alys fought her way into a baker's and confectioner's shop. Greengrocery they bought together too.

"Well, that seems to be everything," gasped Alys as

they piled all their purchases on to the back seat of Richard's car.

"There's just one more thing," said Richard. "I won't be a minute. Just you wait here in the car. Have a chocolate while you're waiting."

He dropped a half-pound box on her lap and disappeared. Alys looked after him, a mist of tenderness in her eyes, the chocolates unheeded. How dear he was. How absolutely wonderful it had been, shopping with him like this. And how perfectly natural it seemed. At least, to her. Had he any idea just how much he meant to her? She tried not to dwell on whether she meant anything to him beyond ordinary liking. He gave no indication of anything else. Valiantly she tried to curb her imagination, to stop herself from contemplating on how wonderful it would be to be doing this with him every Saturday morning like the many young married couples they had seen. She tried to guess where he had gone, what it was they had forgotten.

He appeared suddenly from behind, carrying the most gorgeous bouquet of flowers.

"Here you are," he said, thrusting them into her arms. "No woman and no home is complete without them."

"Oh, Richard!"

For a moment she could not trust herself to say more, or even to look at him. Her lips trembling, she bent her head to the blossoms, smelling their fragrance, gently touching the soft petals. She wanted to laugh and cry at the same moment. After what seemed like an age she found her voice.

"Oh, Richard, they're beautiful. Thank you very much indeed. What a lovely thought."

He flashed her a smile as he manoeuvred the car out of a close-packed line in the car park.

"Thought you'd like them, somehow. And what's the betting that when it was too late, you'd have looked round at the flat and suddenly realised what was missing?"

She wondered, ruefully, what had been his main motive for buying them. For her or for the flat? But whichever it was, the act endeared him to her all the more, and she felt a strong urge to reach over to him and kiss him, to rest her head on his shoulder. But by now, fortunately or unfortunately, he was inching the car through the thick of the Saturday traffic, and to divert his attention by any such means might have been disastrous in one way, at least.

They had a late cup of coffee at the flat, then together, they put away the groceries, and while Alys made preparations for lunch Richard unpacked Alys's trunk, the contents of which consisted mainly of books, pictures and various ornaments and so on. Richard seemed thoroughly to be enjoying his task. He kept up a continuous stream of comments on her choice of books. "Heavens above—what on earth do you see in this author?" Or: "I didn't know you were interested in philosophy."

"Oh yes. Philosophy, history, English literature—why not? There are so many things in the world to be interested in, don't you agree?"

"Hmm. If only one had time."

Alys was silent. Was this more veiled criticism of her job as Home Sister? That this was an easy, soft job, leaving her plenty of time for hobbies and other interests? She crossed to the sink and looked down into the street, and was just in time to see her father's cream-coloured saloon car glide up to the kerb.

"He's here!" she called out excitedly to Richard, her nagging thoughts about what he might be thinking of her put to flight.

She ran downstairs and threw herself into her father's arms as he stepped out on to the pavement.

"Father, how good to see you!"

Tall, upright, his abundant hair now greying, her father held her close to him.

"It's good to see you, too, my dear. How've you been, eh? Let me look at you." He held her at arm's length and eyed her shrewdly as well as fondly. "You're looking very well. Quite blooming, in fact."

She laughted under his scrutiny. "Come on up. Lunch is ready and waiting. And there's someone I'd like you to meet."

"Oh, is there? Is that why you're looking so radiant?"

She coloured. "Now Father—no, it isn't. Richard and I are friends, that's all. And I mean that."

He took his suitcase from the boot of the car. "All right, all right. I understand. Lead me to him."

She laughed, knowing full well that he did, and hand in hand she and her father mounted the stairs to where Richard was just putting the last of her books on the bookshelf. A little shyly she introduced the two to each other, and a little solemnly, they shook hands, sizing each other up.

"Glad to meet you, my boy."

"And I'm more than delighted to meet you, Mr. Newton."

John Newton nodded, then glanced round the room. "Not a bad little place you've got, Alys. A trifle small, maybe, and you could do with some decent furniture, but I expect you've got used to poky rooms at that hostel of yours, or whatever you call it."

"Nurses' Home, Father," she corrected. "And this flat is quite big enough for one, I assure you."

He inclined his head. "For one, for a short time, I suppose."

Alys laughed and showed him into the spare room and told him where the bathroom was, then put on the sideboard the ham and salad and the pair of barbecued chickens she had bought. As hors d'oeuvres she was serving egg mayonnaise for her father and Richard, and melon cocktail for herself. For a sweet, she had prepared fresh fruit salad to a favourite recipe of her father's, containing grapes and dates as well as the more usual fruits.

Richard and her father appeared to get on well together. They chatted easily at lunch, and joined forces in teasing Alys from time to time.

"My boy, I'm glad to see my daughter has got somebody to keep her in order when I'm not around. She's a bit of a handful, I can tell you."

Richard grinned. "I know. She has no respect whatsoever for her elders and betters."

"You've found that out already, have you?" returned her father. "She won't do a thing I tell her."

Now Richard shook his head in mock despair. "And you should hear the cheek she gives me!"

Alys's lips twitched into an amused smile. "Would you two like me to go out of the room so that you can discuss me more freely?" she queried.

Richard raised his eyebrows and looked at her slowly. "Good heavens, Alys, I didn't realise you were here. Do you mean to tell me you've been sitting there all the time?"

Alys suppressed her laughter and made a threatening gesture with one of the salad servers.

Her father roared with laughter, while Richard just sat there and grinned unconcernedly. Alys felt it was all very heartwarming, and she was glad that the two of them were getting on so well together.

"I like that young man of yours," her father said later when Richard went out of the room for a few minutes.

"I'm glad you do. But he's not my 'young man.' I told you, we're only friends."

Her father laughed disbelievingly. "Nonsense! Anyone can see the man's in love with you."

Alys's heart gave an uncomfortable start. "You're imagining things, Father."

John Newton eyed his daughter shrewdly. "Am I? Am I also imagining that you're in love with him?" She made no answer, but gazed through the window unseeingly. "Never mind, my dear, it will all work out, you'll see," finished her father.

She smiled briefly. "He sees more of one of the other Sisters in the hospital than he does of me. And I'm more friendly with one of the surgeons. Richard and I only get together now and again."

Her father shrugged. "Well, I suppose it's more interesting to drag the affair out. But to my mind, it's just a shocking waste of time."

Richard came back into the room just in time to hear the last sentence.

"What's a waste of time?"

Alys held her breath. Surely her father wouldn't—

"I was just saying—what a shocking waste of time it is when two people are in love and they dither about hiding their feelings from each other," he said smoothly.

Alys glanced swiftly at Richard, but his face gave away nothing. At least, nothing which might have made Alys happy. He appeared to think for a moment before saying:

"And what brought up a delicate question like that? Is Alys—"

"I was telling Father about someone I know," she put in swiftly. "But now I think it's time to change the subject. Come and look at the car Father is going to let me have, Richard."

He rose at once, as though he, too, welcomed the change of subject.

"Take Richard for a run," John suggested. "I'm going to have a nap. That excellent lunch you served up—plus the journey—has made me sleepy."

"Yes, Father, all right."

She dropped a kiss on his forehead, and she and Richard went out. Richard was very impressed with the car.

"It's almost new, Alys. Your father must be quite affluent."

"He has a good business," she said evasively.

"Have you driven this particular car before?"

"Yes. When I was home last year." She slipped into the driving seat and he settled in beside her. "Where shall we go?"

He shrugged. "Up to you. I'm just going to sit back and enjoy—or not enjoy—the drive, as the case might be."

She gave a glance over her shoulder before releasing the handbrake and moving off.

"I suppose you're going to sit there criticising my driving?" she said tartly, and silently making up her mind that so far as she was capable she was going to give him no opportunity of finding fault.

It had been almost nine months since she had been behind the wheel. For the first quarter of an hour or so, she drove extra cautiously, then as she regained her confidence and they reached a good stretch of road, she gradually increased her speed.

"Good goer," Richard commented.

"Yes. Like a bird. And brakes, clutch and everything are in tip-top condition."

"Why does your father want to get rid of it?"

She smiled. "I don't suppose he does. I said I was going to buy a second-hand car and straight away he said he was having a new one and I could have this. He wanted to buy me one, but I wouldn't let him do that. What do you imagine this would fetch on the car market, Richard?"

He named a sum she couldn't possibly afford. "You could have bought one of the new mini-cars for the same price—or cheaper," he told her.

"Father doesn't approve of mini-cars. He says the driver doesn't stand a chance in an accident. The bodywork is too flimsy."

After about an hour's driving, Alys ran the car into a lay-by and invited Richard to take a turn at the wheel. He did so and pronounced its performance faultless.

"It wouldn't surprise me if he hasn't just had a complete overhaul. Your father is very good to you, isn't he?"

She nodded. "He'd spoil me completely, if I let him. I'm an only child."

She told him about her mother and other things about herself, and Richard listened in silence. Then when she had finished, he said:

"That fur coat you wore the first time I ever saw you. Was that a present from your father?"

"Yes. I have to be terribly careful not to hurt his feelings. Showing independence is all very well, but there's no virtue in it if it hurts someone else."

"No, I suppose not," he said tersely.

She gave an inward sigh. It was obvious that he did not approve of taking expensive presents from one's parents or parent. He did not understand, of course, just how much money her father made in his business, and somehow she did not want to tell him. At least, not yet.

When they arrived back at the flat her father was just waking up.

"Had a good sleep, Father?" she asked, smiling.

"Wonderful. And how did you get on? Found the old car in good shape, did you?"

She tweaked his ear. "You know perfectly well I did.

Old car indeed! You've had it serviced, haven't you?"

"No more than ordinary, my dear. I always have my cars regularly serviced, you know that. Can't do with breaking down, so inconvenient. And what did you think of her driving, Richard?"

Richard grinned. "Not bad. With a little more practice she might even be quite good."

Alys pulled a face at him and went into the kitchen to make some tea. Later, they went out to dinner, and her father insisted on paying the bill in spite of Richard's strong protests. They had coffee at the flat, and it was turned midnight when Richard announced that he really must be going. He had made several previous attempts to go, but each time John Newton had pressed him to stay longer.

"Goodnight, Mr. Newton. It's been great meeting you," he said. "Are you coming downstairs to see me off, Alys?"

"I suppose I'd better, or we'll never be rid of you," she teased.

He laughed and ran down the stairs before her. But outside he stood beside his car and put a hand across her shoulders.

"Thanks for letting me come and meet your father, Alys. It's been great fun, and I've enjoyed it."

"So have I, Richard."

She thanked him for helping her with her luggage. "I hope you'll come again to the flat. Just drop in any time you feel like it."

He looked at her quizzically. "Any time? Suppose you happen to be entertaining someone else? Chalmers, for instance?"

"I'd still be pleased to see you."

"Hm." He appeared doubtful. "I'm quite sure he wouldn't appreciate my intrusion."

She wanted to tell him that there was nothing special

in her friendship with Ben, that it was he whom she loved, but how could she?

His hand tightened on her shoulder. "Well, I'd best be going, Alys. Thanks again."

It was a warm night and there was a stillness in the air, a certain something in the atmosphere. A precious moment, a feeling of eternity, of timelessness.

"Goodnight, then, Richard," she murmured.

He turned her round to face him and kissed her, and Alys held her breath as his lips touched hers, firm and cool. She felt his arms tighten about her for a moment, then he let her go with something that sounded like a sigh.

"I must go, before I spoil my party manners. Thanks for the lunch and everything. It's been a real pleasure to meet your father—and you're lucky to have such a wonderful parent."

" 'Night, Richard—"

Then, with a final wave he was gone. Alys stood for a moment, the imprint of his kiss still on her lips and a great longing for his love in her heart. Her eyes misty, she turned and went indoors again.

Her father returned to London by train the following evening. When he had gone Alys felt lonely and restless, and with a slight feeling of panic she wondered if, after all, she had done the right thing in deciding to live out. Though she had often been alone in the Nurses' Home, she had never felt lonely. There had been the impression of liveliness all around, the nurses' voices, their laughter, doors opening and closing, the sound of music. Mrs. Wells was so quiet, Alys concluded she must be out. But she knew in her heart that her feeling of loneliness was not so much due to a lack of company as a longing for Richard, an emptiness that only he could fill.

She was glad when Monday morning came and she got into her car and drove herself to the hospital. As she went along she recalled with a fond smile how her father had tried to dismiss her queries as to how much she was to pay him for the car, then when she insisted, mentioned a ridiculously low sum.

"That's all a dealer would allow me, my dear," he told her.

Remembering the figure Richard quoted, she shook her head. "Honestly, Father, if a dealer offered you that, would you take it?"

He sighed. "Honestly—no. But, dash it all, you're my only daughter."

She added another hundred pounds and made him out a cheque, which, after some argument, he accepted.

"I'm still not cleaned out, Father," she told him. "I saved quite a bit—thanks to you—when I was off sick. Remember I was getting full pay and not spending any."

He shook his head at her and very reluctantly put the cheque in his pocket.

"Of course, I know why you're doing this—and I must admit I admire your independent spirit, bless you."

Alys knew that she had still got a good, extraordinarily inexpensive car, and it had pleased her father to let her have it. Her mind now winging ahead to her job, she wondered if there had been any more incidents of missing property, and was pleased to hear, on reporting to Matron, that there had not been.

"There is, however, a nurse in sick bay. I told you, Sister, you're not long without a patient. It's nothing serious, though. Boils. One on the wrist and a couple in the axilla. Dr. Kent saw her yesterday afternoon and referred her to Mr. Chalmers. I asked him to see her when you arrived back on duty, so I expect he'll be along presently. Meanwhile Dr. Kent said she was to stay in bed and have a special diet."

"No penicillin, Matron?"

"No. He's probably leaving chemotherapy to Mr. Chalmers."

Matron asked her if she were settled in all right at her flat, then after a few minutes' chat, Alys was dismissed.

The nurse suffering from boils was one of the newest batch of student nurses, the same nurse who had discovered Edna Farrel after her fall. Alys found her looking pale and uncomfortable.

"Well, Nurse Amos? Let me have a look at these boils of yours." Nurse Amos held out her wrist. The boil was hard and inflamed with a central area of slough. "Good heavens, Nurse, that's one of the worst I've ever seen! Why on earth didn't you report it before? Do you get them often?"

"Well, no, not really, Sister."

"Let me see the others under your arm. Hmm. Not as big as the one on your wrist, but in a very awkward place. All three of them have been giving you quite a good bit of pain, I expect."

"Yes, they have. I hardly slept the night before last. But last night Dr. Kent gave me some Veganin." Alys told her that Mr. Chalmers would be coming over to see her. "Does that mean he's going to—to open it?" Nurse Amos didn't seem to like the idea.

"We'll have to wait and see, Nurse."

But when Ben came he ordered a disc of Elastoplast to be placed over the boils.

"Make a hole in the centre, Sister, and replace it every four or five days. I don't hold with opening up. With penicillin and the Elastoplast you'll find it will come to a head and heal of its own accord. I understand Dr. Kent has put her on a nourishing diet and kept her off duty. That's fine. She's probably run down."

He gave Nurse Amos a swift smile and said he'd

come to see her again in two or three days' time, then wrote up five hundred thousand units of penicillin to be given intramuscularly every six hours.

Alys saw him to the door of the Home. He asked her if she had enjoyed her weekend, and rather conscience-stricken about him, she told him about Richard's offer of a lift with her luggage.

"I almost rang you up on Sunday, Ben," she told him. "I felt awfully lonely after Father had gone."

"Why didn't you? Ring me, I mean?" he asked quietly.

"I hardly liked to. I—thought you might have other plans."

He eyed her gravely. "You're quite sure you wanted to see me, Alys?"

"Ben, of course. We'll be able to see more of each other, actually, now that I've got my own place. It's only half an hour's run."

She told him when her next long evening off duty was and invited him to supper.

"I'd like you to see the flat—really. And," she added hastily, not wanting to hurt him. "I'd like to see you, too."

He smiled then. "You're very, very sweet, Alys. Right. See you Wednesday then. I'll be along about seven, if I'm not held up. If I am, I'll try to ring you."

It was afternoon tea-time. Two Sisters were approaching the entrance to the Home as Ben strode away. One of them was Olivia Longford. Alys spoke to them, but received only the briefest of replies in return. She was not really surprised at this from Olivia. Olivia had never liked her, and had liked her even less since they had both become friendly with Richard. But she was surprised at the other Sister, with whom she had always been on the best of terms. Was it possible that Olivia was poisoning the other's mind against her?

But during the next few days, Alys noticed some of the other Sisters looking at her rather oddly. This puzzled her quite a bit, so that as soon as an opportunity arose, she tackled one of the Sisters who had been in the same class as herself, and with whom at one time she had been very friendly.

"Look, Harris, what on earth's going on? What's the matter with everybody? Something's being said about me behind my back, isn't it? I know the signs. I haven't been in hospital all these years for nothing."

Sister Harris looked most uncomfortable. "I wouldn't pay any attention to it, if I were you, Newton. It's just gossip."

Alys frowned unhappily. "But what is it? Surely you can tell me? After all—"

Sister Harris gave a sigh. "Well, if you must know, it's about these missing articles. Some of them seem to think—I mean—well, dash it all, Newton, *somebody's* been taking the things, haven't they?"

Alys stared at her. "You mean they think the culprit should have been discovered by now?"

"Well—yes, that's right." She rose. "Some of the things have turned up again, I admit, but not all, and some of the Sisters are beginning to remember other things that they've missed but haven't mentioned because they thought they had just lost them somewhere."

"Matron's reluctant to bring in the police, and you can hardly blame her. It wouldn't be very nice at all," Alys said worriedly.

There came another odd look from Sister Harris. "I think it would be better all round if they *were* called in."

"I'm afraid that next time anything is missing, they will be," Alys assured her. "But I'm hoping there won't be a next time."

But this was a vain hope, and the next victim turned

out to be Olivia. She did not report her loss to Alys, but went straight to Matron. Missing from her room, she declared, were a pair of earrings, a present from some-one, and she demanded police investigation immedi-ately.

"This is really serious, Sister," Matron told Alys. "I'm afraid there is nothing else for it. I shall have to report the matter to the police."

"Yes, Matron," Alys said dully.

Matron eyed her with a new keenness. "You know, Sister, I sometimes get the feeling that you have some idea who the culprit might be—that you're trying to protect someone."

"Oh, no, Matron," she denied swiftly.

But it was vaguely true. She had had so many sus-picions of Nurse Farrel, so much evidence had pointed her way, and yet, in some queer way, she wanted to pro-tect the girl.

Matron sighed. "Well, whoever the culprit turns out to be, I'm quite sure we're not going to like it. And, of course, she will have to be asked to leave—whether it's a cleaner, a nurse or—even a Sister."

Alys left the office with a distinct feeling of uneasi-ness. Matron had looked at her oddly when she had said *even a Sister*. Had she someone in mind herself? It was all very worrying and very disquieting, not to say un-pleasant.

A youngish man came from the police, not looking at all like the detective-sergeant he introduced himself as. He listened, his face devoid of expression as Alys began from the beginning and told him about the various inci-dents and the manner of their reappearance. She did not mention Nurse Farrel's name at all.

"Who else—besides yourself—has access to the rooms of the staff, Sister?"

"Why, no one."

"The cleaners?"

"Well, I—of course, many of the nurses and Sisters don't even bother to lock their doors. I have a master key, and if any room does happen to be locked and the cleaners want to do out the room I unlock it for them."

"I see. You supervise the work, of course?"

He asked numerous questions about the estimated time the thefts took place, and about the night staff. Then he interviewed Olivia and got a description of the missing earrings.

"This room—" he said, glancing round Alys's sitting room after Olivia had gone. "Is it one used exclusively by yourself?" She told him it was, more or less. "You have no other room?"

"No, not now. I've recently rented a flat and live out now."

"I see."

He strolled around the room thoughtfully, idly picking up small objects, examining them and putting them down again. There were quite a number of little nick-nacks in the room, mostly little gifts brought back from holiday by the nurses. Some were rather crude, but Alys never could bring herself to throw them out, and she had not wanted to strip the room entirely when she moved into her flat. One particular item was a doll's china cup and saucer with the inscription, "A present from Blackpool," proclaiming its origin in bright gilt lettering. The detective-sergeant picked up the tiny cup —placed upside down on the saucer. He held up something.

"Are these yours, Sister?"

"What, Mr. Maxwell?"

He held out his hand for her to see. Alys stared incredulously. In his palm rested the missing earrings.

CHAPTER SEVEN

"BUT—but this is ridiculous!" Alys gasped.

Mr. Maxwell eyed her stolidly. "They don't belong to you?"

"No, I've never seen them before."

She was sure he didn't believe her. He looked from her to the earrings and back again.

"You said just now that no one else used this room besides yourself."

"That's true. I do sometimes have people in, of course, either to talk to them or to give them tea."

"Do you keep the room locked when you're not here?"

"No, Sergeant, I don't."

Again, that stolid look. "If you've never seen these earrings before, Sister, how do you account for them being here, if nobody uses this room except at your invitation?"

"I have simply no idea."

"Hmm. Well, first, we'd better establish that these actually are the missing items."

"Whosever they are, they're certainly not mine," she told him decisively. "I don't wear earrings."

"That, Sister, is beside the point," he said tersely.

She was about to make an indignant retort, but he put in:

"Will you get Sister Longford here, please?"

With difficulty Alys refrained from arguing with him, much as she wanted to. She rang Olivia's ward, asking her to come to the Home, as the sergeant wanted to see her.

This was a most disturbing turn of events. How on earth had the earrings come to be in that ornament? Alys puzzled as she and the sergeant waited for Olivia to arrive. Surely he didn't really think she was the thief? It was too preposterous. It had not even occurred to her until now, but of all the people who came and went in the Nurses' Home, the one who had the greatest opportunity to purloin other people's property was herself. She alone had access to every room—and right of entry.

The thought gave her a sick feeling in the pit of her stomach and sent shivers trickling up and down her spine.

Olivia came into the room with an air of injured innocence and sweet reasonableness.

"You wanted to see me, Mr. Maxwell?" she all but simpered.

The detective held out his hand in which he had the missing earrings.

"Are these yours, Sister? The ones you say disappeared from your room?"

Olivia let out what could only be called a little squeal of delight.

"Oh, Sergeant, how wonderful! You've found them! I just knew that once the police were called in they'd find out who was really responsible for all these thefts."

She held out her hand for the earrings. But Sergeant Maxwell took out a handkerchief and dropped the trinkets into it.

"Do you mind if I hang on to them for a day or two, Sister?"

She looked at him a little startled. "Why no, Sergeant, if—but I thought you'd found out—I mean—well, Sergeant, I don't want to press charges. Now that I've got my earrings back, that's all I'm worried about."

"I understand, Sister, but there's a little more to it

than that, I'm afraid. The police were called in to investigate these thefts, including yours, and I must pursue the business until I'm satisfied on certain matters. That's all for the moment, Sister. I won't keep you any longer."

Olivia hesitated uncertainly, then with a swift glance at Alys she left the room. The sergeant put the earrings in his pocket.

"You're quite sure, Sister Newton, that you've never seen these earrings before?"

Alys took a deep breath. "Sergeant, I've told you already. I've never seen them before, and I've absolutely no idea how they came to be in my room. If you think for one moment—"

"All right, Sister. What I want to know is, would you be willing to come down to the station with me so that your fingerprints can be taken?"

At the implication in this request Alys felt herself colouring hotly. Nevertheless, she faced him squarely.

"If you really think that's necessary—yes, of course, I'm perfectly willing. I have absolutely—nothing to hide."

If the sergeant noticed her slight hesitation in the middle of her last sentence he gave no sign. Her slight falter had been because she had suddenly remembered Nurse Farrel and the fact that she had told the detective nothing at all of her suspicions.

"Thank you, Sister," he said, moving towards the door. "That's all I wanted to know for the moment. I'll be back to continue my investigations tomorrow."

He was giving little away. Though he had not actually said so, it seemed clear to Alys that he did suspect her. And, thinking the matter over after he had gone, she had to admit that he had grounds for so doing. After all, the missing earrings had virtually been found in her possession.

She wondered if, perhaps, one of the cleaning women had found them one day when she was off duty and popped them in the little saucer for safety, meaning to tell her about them later, then had forgotten all about the things. The only other explanation was that in the words of detective stories, she had been "framed." But the idea was ridiculous. Why should anyone want to do that?

Then all at once she remembered the odd looks she'd been receiving from some of the other Sisters, her conversation with Harris—even Matron. *Whoever the culprit turns out to be, she will have to be asked to leave, whether it's a cleaner, a nurse or—even a Sister.* Alys went cold. *Even a Sister.*

Was everyone suspecting her, then? Even more since the detective had appeared on the scene? It couldn't be true. It just couldn't be.

If it were, she felt she would be quite unable to stay here. She would resign. She determined to see Matron immediately.

But the appearance of Richard in the doorway reminded her that she had a patient. Was it her imagination or did he give her an odd look, too? But all he said was:

"How is Nurse Amos? Or rather how are her boils?"

Alys put her personal problems aside. "Your first question was the better one," she told him. "I'm a little worried about her."

"Why?"

"I know this may sound silly, but she does drink an awful lot—and she's always paying calls."

He frowned. "You're not suggesting—"

"Well, I know it would be just plain silly to jump to the conclusion that every nurse who had a boil or two was a diabetic, but—"

"Have you tested her urine?"

"I haven't the facilities over here."

"All right. Then get a specimen and send it over to one of the wards. More common in men, of course, but we mustn't rule out the possibility. Let's go and see her, shall we?"

Purely professional, nothing personal at all by either word or look, she thought fleetingly as they walked along the first floor corridor to the sick bay.

First, Richard looked at Nurse Amos's boils. "Hm. These under your arm are almost better. What about the one on your wrist?" He eyed the disc of Elastoplast.

"That's much better, too," Alys told him. "This is the second application of Elastoplast. I took the first one off yesterday and pus poured out."

"Good, good. The penicillin is also doing its work, I've no doubt." He glanced at the jug of water on the nurse's bedside locker. "Do you get very thirsty, Nurse?"

The nurse looked up at him. "Yes, I do, actually."

"What's her appetite like, Sister? She doesn't seem to be showing the benefit of that diet I put her on."

Alys told him that she ate very well. Then he asked the nurse about her previous illnesses and about her parents, whether they were both well. Nurse Amos said they were.

He smiled. "All right, Nurse, we'll see how you get on. In the meantime, we'll try a slight change of diet. I'll tell Sister here all about it." Outside, he said to Alys: "No point in saying anything to the girl just yet. I should say she hasn't a clue as to where my questions were leading. If she has got diabetes, it's odd that her medical for superannuation didn't show something of it. Doesn't always follow, of course. Maybe we'd better have a blood sugar even if her urine test is negative."

"It was only an idea," Alys said. "Perhaps I was wrong. There doesn't seem to be any in the family."

"True. Anyway, I'll put her on a high protein diet. Cut down her bread consumption and cut out potatoes altogether. She doesn't need them while she's in bed, anyway. And don't worry about being wrong, Alys. You know the old cliché. Better to be safe than sorry."

She agreed, and they walked down the stairs in silence. Then Richard said :

"I hear you've got detectives in the place."

The observation took her by surprise, and she glanced at him sharply.

"Who told you? Olivia?"

"Well, yes, as a matter of fact."

"There's only been one detective, anyway," she went on raggedly. "And he wouldn't have been here but for her."

Richard raised his eyebrows. "Who can blame her? She was quite upset about the loss of her earrings. Surely anyone would be? What are you so worked up about? I'd have thought you'd be glad to have the thing settled. It can't be very pleasant for anyone to feel there's someone around who can't be trusted to keep their fingers off other people's property."

"Thank you for your opinion, Richard," she said stiffly, "but I can't see that it has anything whatever to do with you."

She hadn't intended to be as rude as that, but he was so obviously on Olivia's side and she was so upset at the idea that she herself was being dubbed the thief, she scarcely knew what she was saying.

"Oh, all right," Richard said carelessly, and walked off without another word.

With a heavy sigh Alys turned to go back to the sick bay. At the bottom of the stairs she came across Nurse Farrel.

"How are you, Nurse?" she asked. "Feeling all right, still?"

"Yes, thank you, Sister. Er—Sister—" Edna hesitated.

"Yes, Nurse, what is it?" said Alys patiently. There was something about this girl that appealed to her. She simply mustn't be branded as a thief. And if she really were that, then Alys was convinced she needed help rather than condemnation.

The girl looked troubled. "Has—has the detective found out anything about the missing things yet, Sister?"

"Why do you ask, Nurse?" Alys asked gently.

"Well, I—I—I mean, I was almost blamed, wasn't I? I just thought I'd ask, that's all."

"Your name has never been mentioned in connection with these missing articles, Nurse," Alys said quietly. "I expect you know about Sister Longford's earrings?"

"Everybody's talking about them."

"I suppose so. Well, they've turned up."

Edna Farrel looked startled. "Oh. Oh, have they, Sister? Is—will—someone be arrested?"

Alys smiled faintly. "I hope not, Nurse. But we'll have to await developments. I'd rather you didn't repeat any of this—but the detective has taken the earrings to the police station with him, presumably to test them for fingerprints."

Edna closed her eyes for a moment. "Oh dear!" she exclaimed.

Alys eyed her worriedly. Did the girl know something about them? She found herself hoping fervently that the nurse wasn't involved. She would almost rather take the rap herself, somehow.

"Is there anything wrong, Nurse? Anything you'd like to tell me?" she asked.

Nurse Farrel looked at her wide-eyed. "No. No, there isn't. Why should there be? I simply know nothing at all about it. Nothing at all."

She darted off, leaving Alys more puzzled and worried than ever. She never dreamed that she would ever have anything like this to deal with when she agreed to the appointment of Home Sister. She would have to report the detective's progress to Matron, of course. Whether or not to resign at the same time, she had not quite made up her mind. Certainly she did not feel she could stay either as Home Sister or anything else in a hospital where those in authority could think for one moment she might be guilty of petty theft.

She went to have a talk with Nurse Amos, first telling her about the diet Richard had ordered for her.

"As well as a nourishing diet he wants you to cut down on carbohydrates, and increase your proteins. You're not getting on as well as he would like. I think you should stop taking sugar in your tea and coffee, too. Too much sugar can cause things like boils, you know." She smiled. "I take a refined form of saccharin myself—helps to keep me slim. You can have some of those. There's absolutely no taste in them—except sweetness."

"Yes, all right, Sister."

It was Alys's intention to find out more about the nurse's parents.

"It's a funny thing about things like taking sugar in tea. It sort of runs in the family, I've discovered. If both parents do, then the rest of the family seem to follow suit. Is it so in yours?"

Nurse Amos looked at her a little sleepily. "Come to think of it, yes. Both my mother and father take two spoonfuls. But they never have boils or anything."

"Don't they? That's interesting. Maybe, as Dr. Kent said, you're a little run down. Tell me, which of your parents do you take after? Most girls like to think they resemble their mother. I'm like my father."

"A bit impossible for me to be like my father. You

see, he isn't my real father. He's my second father—my stepfather. But he's awfully nice. He's just like a real father."

"Do you remember him? Your own father, I mean?"

Nurse Amos shook her head. "He was killed in an accident at work before I was born."

"I see."

This information might be very significant. It could easily be that the girl's own father was a diabetic, and her mother had never mentioned it. Or perhaps the mother had not known. Often a person wasn't discovered to be a diabetic until quite late on in life. Alys made some tea and gave the nurse a cup, complete with sweetening tablets, then drank a cup herself, partly to fortify herself for what might be a difficult interview with Matron. Whatever Sergeant Maxwell discovered from fingerprint tests, she simply could not bear this cloud hanging over her. She must speak to Matron about it.

As it happened Matron saw Alys in her own sitting room, adjacent to her office. She, too, was just having her afternoon tea.

"Sit down, Sister, and have a cup of tea," Matron invited.

This was, at any rate, a good start. "Thank you, Matron." Alys sat down, and after a short interval during which Matron poured out the tea and chatted about the weather, she brought Matron up to date about Nurse Amos, then described how the detective found the earrings.

"But how did they get there, Sister?" said Matron, not unexpectedly.

Alys told her she had no idea. "But you can imagine how I feel, Matron."

"I can indeed."

There was a silence which seemed to Alys to stretch

out interminably. She tried to read Matron's expression, but without success. Then, at last, she said non-committally :

"Well, we shall just have to await developments, I suppose."

But Alys felt she simply could not leave it at that. "Matron, there's something I must say," she began.

"Yes, Sister?"

She took a deep breath. "Am I under suspicion so far as you are concerned? If so, I—I would rather resign immediately."

Matron put down her cup quickly. "Now, let's not do anything hasty, Sister—"

"I'm sorry, Matron, but I must know how you feel, how you regard me. It never occurred to me until today, but suddenly it did. I have more opportunity of —of taking things from the rooms of the staff than any-one else. I have a horrible feeling, though, that it has occurred to some of the Sisters for longer than that."

"What makes you think so, Sister?" Matron asked in a quiet voice.

"Oh, a look or glance here and there, a few words with one of them. Not much to go on, I admit, but I feel I simply can't stay here if I'm not being trusted in my job."

"And have I ever given you any such impression?"

"The other day, Matron, you said that whether it were a cleaner or nurse or a *Sister*, she would have to leave."

Matron smiled. "You're reading into my words some-thing that wasn't there, Sister. Now, I think you'd better go before you say something you will wish you had left unsaid. I shall be as glad as you are when this whole business is cleared up—which I hope will not be long. Oh, and will you do rounds this evening, please, Sister? I shall be in my office the same time as usual."

There was nothing for Alys to do but leave. But she had still not received a straight answer. Was Matron waiting to see the result of the fingerprint test? None of her own would be on, of course. She knew that. But the fact that she was even remotely under suspicion galled her. She told herself not to be unreasonable. Why should she consider herself to be above suspicion? She couldn't really blame either Matron or anyone else. Innocent people were often suspected in these matters. All the same, she hated the idea of being in this position —having access to other people's belongings—if she were not trusted absolutely.

Every ward she visited that evening on her rounds for Matron she was asked about the visit of the detective and whether the culprit had been found. Most of the Sisters were of the opinion that his visit was long overdue.

"Something should have been done about the business ages ago," was a typical remark.

She had to listen, too, to speculations about who the culprit might be.

"You got any idea, Newton?"

Alys shook her head. Not for the world would she mention Nurse Farrel's name in this connection.

"Not the slightest," she murmured.

"It must be one of the cleaners or a junior, surely? A staff nurse or Sister wouldn't be bothered on her salary. Heaven knows, the pay's poor enough, but it's not all that bad that we have to steal. Unless, of course, we've got a sort of kleptomaniac in our midst."

The speaker laughed, as though she hadn't put forward the suggestion seriously.

Alys laughed too, but as she passed on to the next ward, something clicked in her mind. But the idea was so preposterous, she dismissed it. It came back later, however, but as she walked along the ward corridor of one of the male surgical wards a porter was just leaving with an empty stretcher trolley.

"An admission, Nurse?" she asked of the staff nurse in charge.

"Yes, Sister. He's for theatre right away. My only nurse is prepping him now."

"Your only nurse? Short-handed, aren't you?"

"You can say that again, Sister. One has a day off, another an evening, and another is at lecture. The auxiliaries and assistant nurses, of course, went off at four."

Alys picked up the evening report from the office desk. "Well, I'll tell you what, Nurse. I've only one more ward to do. If you like I'll go to theatre with the patient."

The nurse looked vastly relieved. "Oh, Sister, would you, really? Thanks a lot. It's an accident case. Been seen by Mr. Chalmers. Fractured ribs on the right side and emphysema of right chest."

"I'll take his card, Nurse," Alys told her, "and let Theatre Sister have it, then come back for your patient. All right?"

She read the rest of the diagnosis as she made her way to the other ward. The man had been found on the roadside, badly injured, his car nearby. He had a head wound and there was a spreading haematoma over his left groin. His abdomen was rigid and tender and it was likely that he had head injuries. His wife had been informed and signed the anaesthetic consent form, his blood had been taken for grouping and cross-matching and he had had a stomach wash-out, a Ryle's tube being left *in situ*.

Alys collected the report from the last ward, then went to Matron's office to hand in the reports and give her own.

"As Staff Nurse Grainger was short-handed, Matron,

I offered to take the patient to theatre for her," she explained.

"Good idea, Sister," said Matron. She gave Alys a hard look. "Do you ever feel you'd like to go back to ward work? I really think you enjoy doing these rounds, don't you?"

"I do enjoy visiting the wards, yes, Matron," Alys said quietly. "As to whether I'd like to go back—I haven't given it much thought. Were you thinking that it might perhaps be a good thing?"

She felt convinced that Matron was leading up to moving her out of the Nurses' Home and offering her her previous appointment as a ward Sister because of the present nasty situation. But Matron was still not wholly committing herself, it appeared.

"No, no. It was just a thought, Sister. I wondered if you might be getting ready for a change yourself. But we can discuss it some time, if you would like to. Er—thank you, Sister."

This was dismissal, and so there was no more to be said at the moment. But the short interview depressed Alys even more. This was Matron's way of taking her out of the Home because of these thefts. She was convinced of it.

She was almost glad to have her mind occupied by the operation, which Ben performed. He glanced at her in surprise as he saw her at the patient's side.

"Helping out, Sister?" he asked.

She told him she was. "The shortage of staff is as acute as always. Lectures and off-duty time sadly depletes the staff, especially in the evenings."

Ben made a right paramedian incision and found that the liver was ruptured. The spleen was intact, but there was a rent in the serosa and muscle of the transverse colon, and the jejunum was party divided at one point, melaena escaping from it. Ben closed the rents, but could find no cause for the melaena. He closed the abdomen, then in order to investigate the haematoma and swelling in the groin, he made another incision in the left inguinal region. Here, the external iliac vein was found to be damaged, and this was ligated and a drain inserted. A blood transfusion was set up as soon as the patient's grouping was known.

"Are you taking the patient back to the ward, Sister?" asked Ben. She said she was. "Well, tell whoever is in charge to watch his wound carefully and to take his pulse and blood pressure half-hourly, will you?"

"Do you want him specialised, sir?"

"Shouldn't be necessary. I'll be along to see him on the night round."

By the time Alys had seen the patient in bed again, placed on his right side, the night nurses had taken the place of the day nurses.

"Mr. Chalmers said there was no need for a special," she told the senior of them. "But I should stay with him for a while, if I were you, and let your junior get on with the routine work."

"Yes, Sister."

Before she went back to the Nurses' Home to get her outdoor clothes. Alys called in Night Sister's office to tell her about the patient. She did this, then chatted for a few minutes. Sister Halesworth was almost the only senior who, that day, had not asked her all about Sister Longford's missing earrings and the presence of the detective. Alys thought it odd, really. Was it because she didn't know or didn't want to talk about it? She decided to find out, if possible.

"Did you hear about Longford's earrings, Sister?" she asked.

The night Sister looked genuinely surprised. "No. What about them?"

"Well, she sort of lost them. They were missing from her room."

At best, Sister Halesworth had very little colour, but it seemed to Alys that she went even paler.

"What do you mean—missing from her room? Do you mean they were—stolen?"

Alys nodded. "That's what Longford calls it. In fact, it was she who insisted on the police being called in. I've had a detective in the Home all day. He's coming back tomorrow."

"Well, I—" Sister Halesworth began, then broke off abruptly. She drew herself up and squared her thin shoulders. "Well, it's nothing to do with me, Sister, and I must get on with my work, so—"

Alys wished her goodnight and left. There was certainly something unnatural in the night Sister's manner. Was she shielding someone—Nurse Farrel, perhaps? It was all very difficult and unpleasant, and Alys tried to forget about the whole thing as she drove home to her flat. She felt there was nothing to be gained at this point by racking her brains, anyway, and she might just as well shelve the matter until tomorrow.

At ten o'clock the following morning the detective put in an appearance. He declined Alys's invitation to have a cup of coffee—a fact which she felt was ominous—and stood in her office, his hands in his pockets.

"I'd like to see Sister Longford this morning, Sister," he said.

"Why, certainly. I'll get her over for you." She rang Olivia's ward, then asked: "Will you require to take my fingerprints, Mr. Maxwell?"

"Er—no, Sister, I don't think so. Just give me about five minutes alone with Sister Longford, if you don't mind, then I'll have another word with you."

Olivia appeared, and with her was Richard. Alys looked at him in surprise.

"Good morning, Dr. Kent." She stepped out into the corridor, leaving Olivia in the office with the detective. "And what can I do for you?"

"I've come to see Nurse Amos," he said, adding, with a touch of the banter he had not used for a little while : "I trust you have no objections?"

She coloured a little. For the moment she had almost forgotten about her patient, though of course she had seen Nurse Amos since coming on duty.

She told him what she had found out about the girl's father.

"Hm. Then it could be that he was a diabetic," he said. "I got the report of her urine test from Sister Hunt, and I'm afraid that what you feared—what we both feared—is undoubtedly true. There was two and a half per cent sugar. I think she'd better be transferred over to the hospital. She'll need to have four-hourly urine tests, a blood sugar and all the rest of it."

"Poor Nurse Amos!"

"Yes. Still, it's a good thing we discovered it. Two and a half per cent isn't excessive. We might be able to get her balanced with diet alone, but even if she has to go on daily insulin, she'll get as much used to it as putting on her lipstick. We mustn't give her the impression that she's got something dreadful."

"I agree."

Richard explained to the nurse as kindly as he possibly could.

"How far have you got in your Anatomy lectures, Nurse?" he began.

"Oh, we've gone on more to Physiology now, Doctor," she told him proudly.

"Good. Tell me what you know about the pancreas, then."

Nurse Amos told him its position in relation to the other organs, particularly the spleen and duodenum and about the external, pancreatic juice, then about the internal secretion of insulin, which was what Richard was leading up to.

"And what are these cells called which secrete insulin?" he prompted.

Nurse Amos frowned in concentration. "Oh, it's a funny name. Actually we haven't got to that part yet. They're called the—er—islands of something or other. Laverham's, or Langerman's or something."

"The islets of Langerhans," Alys supplied.

"Oh yes, I knew it was something like that."

"And what happens when these islets of Langerhans fail to secrete insulin?" asked Richard.

"Well, then the person has sugar diabetes."

He nodded. "Diabetus mellitus. But you've arrived at it by a short cut, haven't you? Insulin helps the liver to store sugar ready for when the body needs it. When there's no insulin, the sugar a person takes in can't be stored, and it just goes to waste in the urine. This causes a person to drink a lot to get rid of the excess sugar, the body burns up fats instead of sugar causing wasting, and can, if not treated by either diet or insulin, or both, lead to emaciation and general weakness—even coma. But if a person is discovered to have this deficiency in time there's nothing to worry about. The majority of diabetics can live a normal life like anyone else." He paused.

Nurse Amos stared at him, then looked at Alys. There was the beginnings of understanding in her eyes. Richard sat on the edge of the bed, then said gently:

"We think, Nurse, that your islets of Langerhans may not be functioning. You have these boils, which are a symptom, you have excessive thirst, the nourishing diet I put you on hasn't done you a ha'porth of good, and, most indicative of all, your urine test shows positive to Fehling's."

"You mean I—I've got diabetes, Doctor?"

"Almost certainly. But I'm having you over at the hospital where I can keep a better eye on you, and we'll have you balanced in no time."

Both Sister and doctor looked compassionately at the nurse in the bed for a moment. At first, the girl looked downcast, then her chin came up.

"I'm glad you found out. It's a relief, in a way. I've been feeling so tired and everything, and these boils have been really painful. Now I know what's wrong it can be put right, can't it?"

Alys was aware of infinite relief that the girl had the courage and intelligence to look at the matter so sensibly. Richard stood up.

"You bet your sweet life it can," he said, his own relief showing in his voice. "All right, then. I'll see about an empty bed on one of the wards for you." Nurse Amos thanked him, but he shook his head. "Don't thank me, thank Sister here. It was she who first had the suspicion."

The brown eyes swivelled to Alys, then suddenly the nurse's brow furrowed.

"Sister, I shan't have to give up nursing, shall I?"

A swift glance was exchanged between Alys and Richard. Alys shook her head with a gentle smile.

"No, Nurse, I don't think so. Do you, Dr. Kent?"

"We'll see you through your training all right, Nurse, don't you worry."

"Thanks."

Richard left then, and Alys saw him off, her heart full of admiration and compassion for the girl.

"Quite a game kid, isn't she?" Richard observed with a mildness which failed to deceive Alys.

She nodded. "Hope you don't have too much difficulty in stabilising her metabolism."

"I'm not anticipating any. I'll let Chalmers know, by

the way, but the boils are almost cleared up now, any-way."

It seemed to Alys that a sudden chill had crept into his voice. They reached the door of the Home and he left with barely a nod. Alys sighed, and reluctantly made her way back to her office, wondering whether Olivia had gone, and what the detective had had to say to her.

She almost collided with Olivia, actually, and the hostile glare she received as the other left the office chilled Alys to the bone.

CHAPTER EIGHT

DETECTIVE-SERGEANT Maxwell turned as Alys came into the office.

"Well, Sister, I think we've cleared up the little matter of the earrings," he said. "And I shan't require your fingerprints, after all."

Alys looked at him, puzzled. "You mean you've found out who took them?"

He nodded. "And who put them in your office. However, it's the other thefts I'm most concerned about."

Alys frowned. "Perhaps—they weren't really thefts, Sergeant. Every one of the missing articles turned up again. But for the incident of the earrings I don't suppose you would have been called in at all."

He gave her a searching look. "That may be, Sister, but the fact remains the police *have* been called in to investigate."

"But perhaps all these cases of apparent thefts were just instances of carelessness. People leaving their belongings lying about."

The detective eyed her in silence for a second or two, then he said in a casual tone:

"Tell me, Sister, where did you get your china tea-set?"

"It was—a present from my father. He travels a lot. He brought it from the Far East."

"You're fond of your father?"

"Of course."

"So you would value a present from him."

"Naturally."

She wasn't quite sure what he was driving at, unless—

"In that case, Sister, you'd hardly be likely to leave one of the cups and saucers lying about for just anyone to pick up, would you?"

She stared at him. "Why, no. I didn't leave them anywhere. They must have been taken from my room."

"And then put back," the detective stated flatly. He thought for a moment. "There's something very odd about all this business, Sister," he went on. "Discounting Sister Longford's earrings, all the missing items, with the exception of your cup and saucer, were things which were left in the laundry rooms, as though someone took the things on impulse, perhaps, or to teach the owners a lesson. Why do people steal? Have you ever wondered, Sister?"

She shook her head vaguely. The detective was almost chatty all at once. Why? Was he leading up to something?

"I've—never really thought about it," she answered. "Sometimes people are driven to it from need—necessity, I suppose. Like people who steal food or who need something they can't afford."

"Or are too mean to buy?" Mr. Maxwell prompted.

"Yes, I suppose so. There is, of course, the professional thief. The person who regards it as his—or her—living. But that can't apply to anyone here."

"No, I agree. But there's another type of thief. The compulsive thief. The kleptomaniac."

Two people came swiftly to Alys's mind. She wouldn't like either of them to be branded as a thief.

"The person who steals because she can't help it? In that case, surely the person is more in need of help than conviction?"

"Perhaps. In any event these thefts must be stopped —if thefts they are. Now, Sister, how many people knew about this china of yours and knew where it was kept?"

The question caught her off guard. The only two people whose names sprang to her mind were ones she did not want to mention at all.

"I—I don't know, Sergeant. A good many people, I suppose. I'm afraid I can't really help you. In fact, I'd rather you forgot all about my missing articles altogether. They were returned, and that's all that matters as far as I'm concerned."

"But not as far as I'm concerned," the sergeant said quietly. He gave her a penetrating look. "Are you sure you're not trying to protect someone, Sister?"

She drew a swift breath. Was he so discerning, or could it be that he suspected herself? Perhaps he thought she had made a pretence of having her own cup and saucer stolen in order to make herself appear to be one of the victims.

"If—if you don't mind, Mr. Maxwell, I'd like to go and get on with my work now. If—if there was any way I could help you, I would."

He sighed a little. "I hope so, Sister, if only for your own sake. Obstructing the police can be a very serious matter. I hope you realise that."

Alys felt the beginnings of anger. "Sergeant, I've told you all I can. Now may I please go? I have a nurse patient in the sick bay."

"A nurse in sick bay?" he asked sharply. Then : "All right, Sister. I'll have another look round, then go over and see Matron."

Her nerves frayed, Alys left him. She would be glad when this whole thing was over. If only the sergeant would decide there wasn't enough to go on and abandon the case. If only the whole business hadn't even started. She felt angry with Olivia, angry with the detective, angry with herself and with everyone. She knew in her heart that the sooner the real culprit was found the better for all concerned. Even if the detective were to abandon the case there might be more outbreaks later, and they would be back where they started.

With the nagging thought that perhaps if she had followed her hunches and played detective herself the whole matter might have been cleared up now, Alys went about her work for the rest of the day. But how did one set about playing detective without spying? What could she have done? The truth was, she found the whole idea distasteful.

She was glad that she was off duty early today. Everywhere she went she seemed to come across Mr. Maxwell. He wandered up and down the corridors, in and out of the various annexes until in the end he upset the cleaning women, too. They came in a body to Alys's office.

"Sister," said their elected spokeswoman, "what we all want to know is : Who does this detective suspect? Are we under suspicion? Because if we are, we're going to hand in our notices, all of us. We don't like it. Some of us have worked here for years, and if anybody thinks we go around pinching the nurses' stuff—"

"Calm down, Mrs. Briggs. I have just as much access to the nurses' rooms and the laundry rooms as anyone else. It will be better for you, me, and for all of us if he does find out who the culprit is. I've told the sergeant none of you would dream of taking anything. It's as bad for me as it is for you, so please don't make things any more difficult by threatening to leave. The detective is only doing his job."

"Sister's right," put in one of the younger cleaners. "In fact it's worse for her than it is for us. She's responsible, and she's here for longer hours than we are."

There were murmurs of "yes, that's true enough," and "let's hope the feller soon finds out, anyhow."

"Do please be patient, all of you," appealed Alys. "I

know how you feel, really I do. But remember, nothing has actually been stolen. I mean—every single thing, so far, has turned up again."

"Yes, funny thing when you come to think of it. You know, I think somebody's playing a little joke—"

"Some joke!"

"And it's not funny."

Mrs. Briggs said: "All right, Sister, as long as nobody thinks it's us what's been takin' the things—"

"Nobody does, I assure you," Alys said.

"Come on then, girls, let's go an' get on with our work. It'll soon be time we knocked off, anyway."

Alys was reminded that she would soon be off duty, too. Today was Wednesday, her early evening, and she was seeing Ben later. He was having supper at her flat. But this visit from the cleaning women caused Alys to think more seriously about the suspicions she had had herself. Much as she hated the idea, was she really being fair to other people in withholding certain things from the detective? Perhaps if she were to go and see Nurse Farrel—

But it was Nurse Farrel's day off and she was out. Alys didn't know whether to be glad or sorry, and called herself a coward. She went off duty. She would see what she could do about it tomorrow. She would also have to report to Matron the unrest of the cleaners. Whether she would be glad or sorry if the detective found out anything concrete she really did not know. If the culprit turned out to be someone utterly unlikeable, it wouldn't be so bad. But Alys could think of nobody who fitted this description. Except perhaps Olivia. But then she was a friend of Richard. More than a friend, most likely, and Alys wouldn't like to see him upset.

Thinking of Oli   eminded her about the earrings. Why hadn't the sergeant told her who had been responsible for taking them from Olivia's room in the first place, then planting them in her sitting room? Had he really found out or not? She felt her cheeks colouring as she remembered her conversation with him, or rather his interrogation. He had asked some very odd questions. She was still suspect, or so it seemed to her.

But her brain felt too tired to think or feel anything very deeply. She drove to her flat and made some tea and put some records on her record player and tried to relax. Then after a while she tidied the flat and changed and began to prepare supper. Prompt at seven Ben arrived. She was more pleased to see him than she had thought she would be.

"You did remember that I was coming, then?" he asked with a rueful smile. "I'd been wondering whether I ought to have rung and reminded you."

"Oh, Ben, really! Of course I remembered. I've been looking forward to seeing you," she said warmly.

She led the way upstairs, thinking it was really quite a time since she and Ben had seen each other out of the hospital. Did he know about the business of the missing property and everything?

"I say, you have got yourself a nice place, haven't you?" he remarked as she showed him over the flat.

"You like it?"

"Very much indeed. One gets tired of having a resident job. As a matter of fact, I've been thinking of casting around for a general practice or a non-resident hospital post."

"Wouldn't you miss hospital life?" she asked.

He sighed. "I don't know. It would depend on— what other compensations there were, I suppose. I'm not ambitious, Alys. As long as I'm doing my job—"

"But, Ben, you have enough experience and qualifications to accept a consultant's position."

He shook his head. "Too specialised. It's difficult to escape specialisation, I know, but—"

She sensed some restlessness, some general dissatisfaction in him. Not all men were careerists. Some were content to jog along in a job they liked and go home in the evenings to a quiet, peaceful home life with a wife and children, and were nonetheless men for that. But even so—

"The average G.P. will tell you that his life is no picnic," she felt bound to remind him.

He lowered himself into one of her armchairs and pulled out his pipe from his pocket.

"It's much better than it used to be, and a darned sight less hectic than hospital life."

"Ben—" She felt a sudden warmth of tenderness towards him and a great desire to comfort him came over her. She sat on the arm of his chair and put her arm across his shoulders. "Ben, you're tired. I've never heard you talk in this way before."

He gave a slight smile and looked up at her. "Alys, you're a wonderful girl."

Something in his voice and in the depth of his eyes made her heart give an uncomfortable leap. Was Ben in love with her? She blinked and gave his shoulders a gentle squeeze.

"You're not so bad yourself. Now, just you relax for a while, Ben, and I'll go and bring in the supper. It's all ready."

On her way to the kitchen she switched on her record player, and in a moment the lovely strains of the *Swan Lake* ballet music filled the flat. Her mind in something of a turmoil she put the chicken *vol-au-vent* she had made on a tray together with the grilled mushrooms and tomatoes.

Ben needed her. She sensed it. He needed her far more than Richard did, who indeed did not seem to need her at all, did not appear even to want her friendship. As she stood, immobile, for a moment, her hands on the handles of the tray she became aware, too, of her own need. She needed love, needed to feel cared for, to feel sure of someone. And here, in Ben, it was being offered to her. They could fill a need in each other.

She took a deep breath and picked up the tray and carried it in.

Ben rose swiftly to his feet. "That looks heavy. Let me take it."

"It's all right—"

But she relinquished the tray and let him carry it the rest of the way to the table.

"Here am I, letting you do all the work. You must have had as busy a day as I've had."

She grimaced and gave a rueful smile. "Not so much busy as aggravating." She set the plates and dishes out on the table and invited him to sit down.

"Hm. It looks marvellous," he said appreciatively. "Don't tell me you can cook, too."

She laughed. "Well, I cooked this, at any rate. But don't speak too soon. Remember, the proof of the pudding—"

"Is in the eating, I know. Hurry up and let me have some. It looks marvellous, and I'm starving."

She served it, and at the first mouthful Ben pronounced it delicious.

"You know, I don't know how we put up with hospital life. Half the time we don't know what we're missing."

"Perhaps it's just as well," she said philosophically. "Anyway, somebody's got to do it."

Over the meal they talked generalities, then, after an orange trifle with dairy cream, Ben insisted on making the coffee. It was when they were drinking it, Ben in an armchair, Alys at one end of the comfortable settee, that he asked her about the affairs of the day.

"You look charming, as usual," he said, "but at times there are lines of worry about your eyes. They tell me you've still got that detective fellow in your hair. What's happening? It must be awfully worrying and unpleasant for you."

"It is, Ben. The more so because I have an idea who's responsible, and also because I'm number one suspect."

"What! Really, that's just too ridiculous. Who suspects you, of all people, for goodness' sake?"

It was good to be able to talk to someone. She told Ben everything, missing out nothing. For a while, he listened in silence, puffing at his pipe. Then presently he left his chair and came and sat beside her.

"Look, darling, nobody worth a second thought would even dream of suspecting you. Remember that. Olivia has a pretty mean streak in her and is capable of the worst kind of jealousy. She probably only pretended to have her earrings stolen and planted them in your sitting room herself. An old trick, but the sort you never expect in real life. She probably didn't stop to think about things like fingerprints, and it's quite likely that only her own were on the things."

Alys gave a little smile. "You're probably right, Ben, bless you. I had a vague idea of something like that myself, but it seemed too fantastic. But what about all the other things? I'm pretty certain Olivia had nothing to do with those."

Ben frowned. "What I can't understand is the way things keep turning up again. Surely even a kleptomaniac wouldn't do that? I'm not sure, but I think kleptos hoard things rather like a magpie does."

This was something Alys had not thought about. "It would almost seem, in view of that, as if one person is doing the stealing, and another is putting them back. The detective thinks I'm shielding someone—which in fact I am, in a way. But suppose somebody else is doing the same?"

"But from what motive?" asked Ben. "There doesn't seem the remotest connection between Nurse Farrel and Sister Halesworth."

"Not enough for one of them to be shielding the other, at any rate." Alys sighed. "I just seem to go round in circles until my head's fit to burst."

Ben put his arm around her. "You shouldn't be having all this to contend with."

She laughed shortly. "One way and another I'm tempted to pack it in and go somewhere else. Whatever you may say, Ben, there are *some* who blame me for what's happening in the Home."

"It's simply disgraceful that you're being made to feel that way." He turned her head round to face him and looked into her eyes. "I love you, Alys," he said simply. "Would you fancy life as the wife of a G.P.?"

She met his gaze steadily. "I'm fond of you, too. It might not be such a bad idea at that. In fact, right now it sounds very, very attractive indeed."

He bent his head and kissed her. "Darling, you're wonderful. I've thought such a lot about you lately. And I can't tell you how jealous I've been of Kent."

She disengaged herself gently from his arms. "However I might have felt about Richard, he thinks precious little of me," she said bleakly.

Ben stroked her cheek. "I wouldn't know about that. It's difficult to see below the surface of a man like him. But I doubt if it's in him to be serious about any woman, and I'm sure Olivia is going to get hurt. So far as she's capable of being hurt, that is." He was silent for a brief moment, then he said quietly: "Tell me, Alys, how *do* you feel about Richard?"

She closed her eyes momentarily. "Don't ask me,

Ben. I don't know. I'm all mixed up. I thought at one time I was in love with him, but—"

"Now, you're not so sure," Ben finished for her. "Well, as far as I'm concerned that's fine. And believe me, I shall do my best to encourage you in the idea."

She smiled and touched his cheek. "You do that, Ben."

She felt she was more than half in love with him already. It was just that when she thought of Richard she wanted to weep and there was a small knot of despair in her heart. Ben was wonderful. So kind and gentle. She allowed him to cradle her in his arms and make a little tender love to her. There was nothing demanding or passionate about him. He was all tenderness, all loving.

She said goodnight to him reluctantly. He kissed her once more as he was ready to go.

"Goodnight, darling. It's been a wonderful evening. Don't come downstairs with me. I'll see myself off. And I'll see you again soon, I hope."

"Yes, Ben. Soon," she whispered.

She must do something about this ache in her heart, must try to forget Richard. It was ridiculous to feel like this about him, anyway. He had never given her the least encouragement to fall in love with him.

There was a message on Alys's desk the following morning. Matron wanted to see her. Full of misgivings, she tapped on the door of her office just after nine o'clock. Matron called to her to enter.

"Good morning, Sister. There's something I want you to do for me," Matron began without preliminary. "I don't know whether you've heard or not, but Sister Thompson was taken ill suddenly last night. At least, a pain in her back which she had been putting up with became so severe, Night Sister had to send for Dr. Kent. I think she has a retroverted uterus. At all events, she's in the side ward of Gynae, and the gynaecologist is seeing her this morning. The point is, Sister, that with Sister Jones already on holiday, this leaves theatre very short of trained staff indeed. I wonder—would you help out? It may only be for a week at most. I wouldn't ask you, but there's simply no one else who can be spared. There's no one in sick bay at the moment, is there? And I'm sure the cleaners will carry on quite happily."

Was this just a ruse to take her out of the Home, the "thin end of the wedge"? Still, if Sister Thompson had been taken ill—

"Very well, Matron. When do you want me to take over?"

"This morning, if you could. I see Sister Thompson was to scrub in general theatre. There's quite a formidable list."

The detective had said he was seeing Matron yesterday. Why had she not mentioned his visit?

"Er—Matron, there's just one thing I feel I should tell you," Alys said. "The cleaning women came to my office yesterday."

Matron glanced up sharply. "All of them, you mean?"

"Yes, Matron. They were unsettled, feeling they were under suspicion about these thefts. I did my best to reassure them. They talked of giving in their notices— *en bloc*. But I told them they were no more under suspicion than anyone else—than myself, for instance."

"And they're happy now?"

"Well—yes, Matron. But—"

"Good," Matron said briskly. "Mr. Maxwell came to tell me what he had so far discovered. I'm afraid he's finding it all very difficult, but I believe he's just going to wander around for the next day or so and keep his eyes open. Then, if nothing turns up, he'll just have to drop the case, that's all." She smiled briefly. "Thank you, then, Sister."

"Thank you, Matron," Alys echoed absently, and went out.

Again, she had been told precisely nothing. And if she were going to be kept busy in theatre, what chance would she have of talking either to Nurse Farrel or Sister Halesworth? She supposed whoever the culprit was, whether either of them or someone she had never even thought about, the person would undoubtedly be too scared to try anything while the detective was about the place. Yet if the culprit was a kleptomaniac would his presence make any difference? She wouldn't have thought so.

From Matron's office Alys went straight to the theatre unit. There were three theatres—urological, orthopaedic and general. Fortunately, there was nothing in the orthopaedic theatre until the afternoon. In the urological theatre a staff nurse was setting-up for an intravenous pylogram, and in general a staff nurse was preparing for the first case of Ben's, a gall bladder operation. A third-year nurse was setting up for the anaesthetic. Alys went to the office and looked at the off-duty list. The third-year nurse had a lecture at nine-thirty. At least two nurses would be required as "dirty nurses."

She was thankful for the six months she had had as theatre staff nurse and also for her period as junior theatre Sister and her time as ward Sister on surgical. She picked up the case card of the first patient on the list and decided to take the instrument trolley herself.

"You'd better go now, Nurse," she told the third-year student. "Otherwise you won't have time for a cup of coffee before your lecture." Alys ran her eye over the anaesthetic trolley. "Who's giving anaesthetics this morning?" she asked the staff nurse.

"Dr. Kent is giving the first one, Sister. Mr. Thorpe is coming later with Mr. Banks for the pancreatectomy and the gastroenterostomy."

Richard. "I see. Well, I think you'd better go on anaesthetics, Staff Nurse, if you don't mind. You're probably more *au fait* than I am there. In fact, you're bound to be, whereas I'm fairly familiar with Mr. Chalmers's methods."

She would probably be able to cope with Mr. Banks, too, but as he was not coming until after lunch, she would be able to look a few things up during her lunch hour, also study the patients' history cards.

She was scrubbing up to lay out the instruments when Richard came into theatre. He stopped short at the sight of her at one of the washbasins.

"Hello, hello, hello! If it isn't the reverend Home Sister," he said mockingly. "What on earth are you doing here?"

Alys felt her whole being tighten. "I think that joke has worn a little threadbare, Dr. Kent," she said icily. "In fact, more than a little."

She did not look at him, but could imagine the way his dark brows would have shot up.

"Dear, dear, we are in a mood this morning, aren't we?"

Alys turned off the taps with her elbows and walked over to the towel drums.

"As to what I'm doing here," she continued as if he had not spoken, "I imagine you know why, since you were called to see Sister Thompson."

"Ah, yes, of course. And I suppose you were the only Sister who could be spared from her job."

Her eyes sparked angrily. "Then it's a fortunate coincidence that I also happen to have had some theatre experience, too, isn't it?"

She dropped the sterile towel into a linen bin and

depressed the pedal of the gown drum. Richard went to a scrubbing-up bowl and picked up a scrubbing brush. At that moment Ben entered.

"Hello, Alys, so they've got you on the job, have they? Good. I heard about Sister Thompson. Is she having her op today?"

Alys's anger vanished. "Hello, Ben. I haven't heard. I believe she's being seen by the gynae man this morning. I expect she could be fitted in this afternoon, if he advises surgery. I'm not sure how urgent it is."

She held the tapes of her sterile gown while one of the nurses tied her into it at the back, then proceeded to put on her gloves. As she went into the main body of the theatre where the autoclaved instruments lay waiting under a sterile towel, she could hear Ben and Richard talking to each other. About the patient, without doubt, she supposed. Richard really was the most aggravating man she had ever met, her thoughts went on as she checked that the general set was complete, plus the additional instruments required for cholecystectomy. The staff nurse, too, knew her job. They were all correct.

She was aware of Richard passing through to the anaesthetic room, but did not look up from what she was doing. She covered the instrument trolley once more with a sterile towel, then attended to needles and sutures.

It was astonishing how one slipped back so easily into another job. But she reflected, as she handed the instruments one after the other to Ben, that she wouldn't like to do this kind of work all day every day over a long period. As well as removing the gall bladder Ben explored the common bile duct in case any stones had become lodged there. Sometimes while he was operating he asked questions of the ward nurses both to help them in their examinations and to make sure that the patient would have the best possible nursing. This morning he asked the nurse:

"What are gallstones, Nurse?"

The eyes over the mask looked a little startled, as if the question had caught her unawares.

"They—they're little stones which collect in the—the bile duct."

"That's not a very good answer, Nurse. It tells me very little. What year are you?"

"Third, sir."

"And when do you sit your finals?"

"Next April."

"Well, Nurse, it's a question you might be asked. It's not the sort of question which, if you don't know the answer, can cause a patient's death or anything like that, but it does show that you've really studied the subject. Apart from that, if you're stumped over a simple question like this it's liable to put you off and make your mind go a blank." He broke off to ask Alys for a bougie, then went on: "Gallstones are always associated with inflammation, Nurse, and are considered to be the result of germ infection, the stone in turn resulting from the deposit of mineral salts round a nucleus of septic material. On the other hand, of course, inflammation can be present without the formation of stones. And the stones themselves, Nurse, consist of cholesterol and bile pigments. If I were you I should look the whole thing up when you go off duty while the operation is fresh in your mind."

"Yes, sir. Er—thank you very much, sir."

Alys saw his eyes twinkle. "Not everyone gets a private lecture, Nurse. Do they, Sister Newton?"

"Indeed, no," responded Alys.

Richard gave a good imitation of a snort. "Perhaps Nurse would like a private lecture on anaesthetics while she's about it."

"It might not be a bad idea at that," Ben said blandly.

But Richard had no intention, it seemed, of asking the nurse any questions about anything. He remained silent, but his dark eyes flicked from Ben to Alys in a kind of angry speculation.

Ben inserted a precautionary drainage and began the process of closing up.

"All right, Nurse, since you're not going to get a lecture from Dr. Kent. Tell me what you know about after-care of cholecystectomy."

"She—should be nursed in a sitting-up position after the effects of the anaesthetic wear off, sir, and watched carefully for post-operative haemorrhage."

"That could apply to almost any operation. Anything else?"

"The—dressing will have to be done every day and the—er—draining tube withdrawn a little and perhaps an inch or so cut off. Then it can be removed about the second or third day. The other one is drained into a bottle."

"What else must you watch out for—apart from haemorrhage? How do you know whether things are working satisfactorily inside, that there is no biliary obstruction?"

"Oh—paling of the stools, sir," the nurse said with a rush.

Ben nodded. "Anything else? What about the urine? Any changes there?" But here the girl was stumped. "It becomes darker, Nurse," Ben told her. "If you're wise, you'll learn all you can about the biliary tract while you have the chance and observe your patient carefully."

"And while you're observing, Nurse," put in Richard pointedly, "don't forget that the patient is a human being in need of your sympathy and understanding *and* reassurance."

The patient having no further need of him for the moment, Richard strolled out of theatre leaving a distinctly uncomfortable silence behind him. Alys felt angry with him. He had implied that Ben was putting too much stress on the aspect of the patient as a case. It was not so at all. Ben had only been trying to help the nurse. He was just as humanitarian in his approach to his work as Richard was. Really, Richard could be infuriating at times.

But Ben said : "What Dr. Kent said is quite right, of course. Any patient is first and foremost a human being, not merely a case to be observed. But one thing is no good without the other. To be a good nurse you must have both sympathy and knowledge. Remember that."

Alys had never admired Ben more than at that moment. In being so honest he had come out best, after all, and made Richard appear almost like a truculent schoolboy. Not that she was overjoyed about the latter. She just couldn't help wondering what had got into Richard.

Alys did not feel at home at all in theatre. She never had been enthusiastic about theatre work, and now felt restless and unsettled. Detective-Sergeant Maxwell was still prowling about the Nurses' Home and seemed no nearer a solution to the problem of the petty thefts. Alys pondered the matter of whether she should have a talk to Nurse Farrel, but couldn't think how to approach the girl. So for a few days, at any rate, the situation was one of stalemate, and all Alys could do was carry on with her work and travel back and forth to her flat, filling in her off duty with purely domestic affairs like shopping and the tidying up. Ben was having a very busy time in theatre, and as Richard only gave anaesthetics on rare occasions she barely saw him at all. He neither rang her, called to see her, or made any attempt to talk to her, and Alys went mechanically about the business of living. How long she could go on like this, she didn't know. Then towards the end of the week, another article of clothing was missing from the second-floor laundry room. A cotton dressing gown. This, it appeared was what the detective had been waiting for.

"And this time, Sister," he said to Alys as she was going towards the Sisters' sitting room, "I have a very good idea who the culprit is."

CHAPTER NINE

ALYS caught her breath. She looked at the detective and felt she heartily disliked him.

"I'm sure we shall all be very relieved when the whole business is cleared up, Sergeant," she said coldly.

"Not all, I'm afraid. There are quite a number of people who *won't* be very happy about it."

"I suppose so. May one ask who—"

He smiled. "No, Sister, one may not. I shall let you know all in good time."

With a nod, he passed on, leaving Alys staring after him exasperatedly. She sighed and changed her mind about going into the sitting room. Who was it the sergeant suspected? Had he really found out? Alys retraced her steps to the front entrance of the Home. Nurse Farrel was coming down the stairs, an untidy bundle in her arms.

"What have you got there, Nurse?" Alys asked, not knowing quite why she did so, unless it was the swift look of fear she detected in the girl's eyes.

Edna glanced at the bundle swiftly. "It's—nothing."

Alys gave a slight smile. "It's hardly nothing, Nurse. It looks to me very much like a dressing gown."

The girl's face grew pink, then her eyes flashed. "All right, so it's a dressing gown. What of it?"

"A dressing gown has recently been stolen, Nurse," Alys told her quietly. "Where did you get that one?"

Nurse Farrel's lips tightened and she took a long, deep breath.

"Will you please mind your own business, Sister?"

She thrust past Alys, almost knocking her down, and

hurried in the direction of her room. But Alys went after her and stepped swiftly into the girl's room, closing the door behind her.

"Now look, Nurse, this is serious. I've just been talking to Detective-Sergeant Maxwell, and—"

"I don't care what you've been doing or what he said. I'm telling you nothing. If he likes to think I've taken it or any of the things that have been missing, he's welcome. I don't care. I don't care if I leave this place tomorrow. I'm sick of it, anyway!" Nurse Farrel sat down heavily on her bed, and folded her arms belligerently.

Alys looked at her, puzzled. "You know that isn't true, Nurse. You like nursing, you know you do."

Edna glared at her. "What do you know about what I like and what I don't like? Why don't you go away and leave me alone?"

There was a break in the girl's voice which she tried desperately to control. Alys dropped on to the bed beside her, convinced, somehow, that this girl was no thief.

"Where did you get this dressing gown, Nurse?" she asked quietly.

Edna took another deep breath. "I'm not telling you."

"All right." Alys picked up the garment from the bed.

Nurse Farrel glanced up sharply. "What are you doing with that?"

Alys moved to the door. "I'm going to take it and put it somewhere where the detective can find it. And when I come back, you're going to tell me who it is you're shielding—and why. Meanwhile, the thing mustn't be found in your room."

Swiftly, she rolled the dressing gown up inside out and opened the door, only to run straight into Detective-Sergeant Maxwell.

"Well, well," he said, his glance going immediately

to the bundle under Alys's arm. "The missing dressing gown, I believe?"

Alys closed her eyes despairingly and sighed. Nurse Farrel gave a gesture of hopelessness.

"You'd both better come to the office," said Mr. Maxwell, "and let's get this thing thrashed out."

Alys turned to Edna. "Come along, Nurse, let's get it over. It has to come out sooner or later, you know."

"What does?" asked the detective as he closed the door behind them and followed them to the Home Sister's office.

"I don't know," Alys said with heavily lined patience. "What I do know is—Nurse Farrel is no thief.".

The girl turned slowly and looked Alys full in the face. The look was one of gratitude mingled with puzzlement, then with a barely perceptible shake of the head she turned away.

In the office the detective suggested that they be seated, taking himself the chair at the desk.

"Now then," he began. "Suppose you tell me what this is all about?" Neither spoke, and the detective looked from one to the other. "Well, let's start with you, Sister Newton. I saw you a few minutes ago and you had nothing in your hands. The next thing, I see you coming out of Nurse Farrel's room carrying the stolen dressing gown. Suppose you tell me where you got it and where you were taking it?'

Alys pounced on a way out without lying. "I was going to—" then she faltered.

"To put it somewhere where I could find it—as you had done so often before?"

"No, I—" Alys began to deny vehemently, but again checked herself. "I'm sorry, Mr. Maxwell, but I'm afraid I can't help you any more."

"Can't? Or won't? Now, listen to me, Sister—and Nurse. Trying to hinder the course of justice by shielding someone never achieves anything, except to postpone the inevitable. You, Sister, are trying to protect Nurse because you don't want to believe her guilty, and Nurse, I suspect, unless she prowls around at two o'clock in the morning, is trying to protect someone else. Between you, you two have made my job very difficult and have helped to draw out this case to the embarrassment of all concerned. Oh, I daresay you meant well, but you really will have to learn to trust the police."

"Trust you to ruin people's lives and their careers!" burst out Nurse Farrel.

"Nurse, *please*—" remonstrated Alys, though she had every sympathy with the girl. She turned to the detective. "Nurse is very outspoken, but she doesn't mean to be rude. It's just that she's naturally honest, and that's why, as you have guessed, I was trying to protect her. I suspected, as you do, that she was trying to cover up for someone else, and it's greatly to her credit. It's—someone on night duty, isn't it?"

"Sister—no!" came from Nurse Farrel.

"It's no use, Nurse, the Sergeant knows, that's obvious." Alys told her gently. "It's—Night Sister, isn't it?"

Sergeant Maxwell eyed her for a moment. "Your loyalty to a colleague does you credit, so does your endeavour to protect a young and innocent girl. Why Nurse, here, has gone to so much trouble to protect a senior is another matter."

He looked to Edna for enlightenment, but was disappointed. The girl's hands were clasped tightly on her lap, and her face showed signs of acute distress, as did her voice when she said:

"I don't know what all the fuss is about. Why can't you leave Sister alone? All the things that were—were —taken were put back. Nobody's really lost anything. She—she doesn't mean any harm. We all got used to her. It was so simple—I mean—" She broke off and looked distractedly from one to the other. "It's all very well for people like you. You've got homes and parents—proper homes, I mean. You don't know what it's like to—"

Alys put a gently restraining hand on the girl's arm. From the impassioned but rather incoherent outburst, it was clear that she already knew Sister Halesworth before coming to the hospital, had probably been brought up in the same institution or foster-home.

"Don't say any more just now, my dear. I'm sure the Sergeant understands."

Sergeant Maxwell nodded, and Alys saw a softness and understanding in his eyes.

"There will be no conviction, Nurse, if that's what's worrying you. The police know all about kleptomania, and they recognise a genuine case when they see one. Such a person is not a thief by intent but by impulse or mental aberration. Sister is not dishonest, she needs psychiatric help. You and Sister Newton, here, and Matron, will be the only people who know, and you can still help Night Sister by doing your best to keep it that way. Now, I must go over and report to Matron."

He went out. Nurse Farrel sat disconsolate, her head bent, her lips pressed tightly together. Alys put her arm around the girl's shoulders.

"Try not to take this too hard, my dear. You did your best and I'm sure you've helped Sister a great deal. Perhaps it's better this way. It was bound to happen sooner or later. You just can't protect someone indefinitely, and she may be better with treatment."

"Will she—have to leave, do you think?"

"It's likely, Nurse. It will be better for herself if she does."

Edna buried her face in her hands. "Oh, how awful! Poor old Lottie. It's not her fault. She was just

abandoned when she was a baby—like me. I ask you—
what chance have any of us got?"

She burst into tears, and Alys let her cry for a minute. Then she said gently :

"My dear, I know how you feel, really I do. But you
know, there are far worse things than having no real
parents. There's having bad parents."

Edna's head shot up. "Even bad parents are better
than none!"

Alys shook her head. "You might think so, but strange
as it may seem—though it shouldn't to you, as you say
you were an abandoned baby—not all parents, mothers,
love their children. It would have been even worse if
your mother had kept you, then ill-treated you or
starved you, not only of food, but of love."

But Edna shook her head vigorously. "I wouldn't
have cared, if only I'd had a real mother."

But Alys felt she had to be firm with the girl. "Listen,
Edna—that is your name, isn't it? You've got to put all
that behind you, otherwise you'll never be really happy.
What you need to do is learn to love other people. That
way, you'll build up love around you. Don't think of
yourself as having an exclusive problem, and don't let
your beginnings mar your life. Almost everybody has
some problem in their lives, or starts off with some dis-
advantage. The thing to do is to turn these things to
your advantage. Even having good parents and a comfortable home can have its drawbacks. It can make a
person selfish and complacent. Don't think I'm trying to
dismiss your bad start in life as of no consequence. I'm
not. I'm only trying to get you to make *use* of it. So
far, you've done remarkably well. You have a stronger
character than many a girl from a normal home background. Just soften up in your attitude a little, that's
all. Be willing to do the same for anyone as you were
for Sister. See what I mean?"

For a moment Edna did not answer. "You've been very good to me, anyway, Sister," she said then. "And I think I know what you mean. You want me to stop feeling sorry for myself, don't you?"

Alys smiled. "That's one way of putting it. There's one thing for sure. I hope that if ever I'm in a spot I've got a friend like you somewhere around."

Nurse Farrel rose. "I've been very rude to you at times, Sister. I'm sorry about that. Thanks for being so willing to keep me out of trouble. Talk about having someone like me around! The boot's on the other foot. It's not going to be easy to stop hitting out at people in authority and feeling I've had a raw deal from life, but I will try."

Alys's hand rested on the girl's shoulder for a moment. That's the ticket. Why not drop in to see me any time you feel like a natter? I'll always be pleased to see you at my flat. Wait a moment and I'll write down my address for you."

Shortly after Nurse Farrel had left Matron rang and asked Alys to go to her office.

"Have you had your tea, Sister?" she enquired.

"Well no, Matron, but—"

"Then come to my sitting room and we'll have some together."

Alys made her way across to the hospital buildings and was just entering the main corridor by a side door as Richard was walking past. His old grin appeared on his face.

"Hello there! Long time no see. Still in theatre—or have you gone back to your seminary?", he asked banteringly.

"Is that all you can think of to say, Richard?" she asked, and realised she had been quite unable to keep the wistfulness out of her voice.

His dark eyes opened a little wider, then he looked at her for a long moment.

"No," he said in a more serious tone. "There are lots of other things I could say, but I imagine this isn't the time to say them. You look as though you're on your way somewhere, and I've had an urgent call to Cavell. Besides—"

Her heart missed a beat. "Besides—what?"

But he shrugged. "Oh, nothing. See you around, Alys. I must go now."

Alys suppressed a sigh and went on her way. She tapped on Matron's sitting room door and was invited to enter. Was it her imagination or had Matron's voice a new warmth? Alys found herself feeling a tiny bit resentful. She had rather have had Matron's confidence completely, and felt like carrying out the cleaners' threat.

"Ah, Sister, do sit down. Tea's all ready to pour. Help yourself to a sandwich or something."

But Alys had no appetite either for the dainty sandwiches or for small talk. The fact the culprit had been found at last brought little or no satisfaction, involving as it did a person in the night Sister's position. But now Matron's voice took on a sober note.

"Well, Sister, I believe you know all about this dreadful business. You'll be glad to have the matter cleared up, I'm sure, but you'll be as sorry as I am about Sister. It's a sad, sad business, and I shall have no alternative than to ask her to leave at once, I'm afraid."

Alys agreed with Matron that it was a very unhappy affair. "I'm glad, naturally, that I'm no longer suspect, but—"

Matron frowned. "Whoever said that *you* were suspect, Sister?"

"I—Well, quite a number of people, Matron. Some of the other Sisters. I feel sure, and even you yourself at one time—"

Matron put down her cup carefully. "My dear child, what on earth gave you that idea? If I'd thought for one moment that you were feeling that way—Please believe me, it never crossed my mind."

Alys suddenly felt ashamed and rather small. "I'm sorry, Matron, truly I am, but I'm afraid I felt pretty much as the cleaning women did. I just didn't want to carry on if there was even the faintest suggestion—and of course, why shouldn't there be suspicion of me? I had every opportunity."

Matron smiled and picked up her tea again. "If I'd realised how you were torturing yourself, I'd have reassured you. But it was a very tricky situation. I had an idea you knew something and didn't want to come out with it, and I must say I admire you for it. Anyway, we'll just say that Sister has been taken suddenly ill—a nervous breakdown, which isn't far off the truth, anyway, and a hint here and there that the police didn't think we had a case—and the whole affair will soon be forgotten. By the way, you'll be able to go back in the Home on Sunday. Sister Jones will be back from holiday by then and if they need any extra help I'll find a staff nurse or a third-year pro from somewhere."

Matron chatted on about hospital affairs in general until Alys felt herself being dismissed. She went back to theatre where Ben was just finishing a double herniotomy. Work in all the theatres was slowing down. Nurses were busy clearing up and preparing for possible emergencies. Alys went to the theatre office to sort things out a little. She needed to sort out her own thoughts, too. She had not given in her notice, after all. From Sunday onwards everything would be back to normal.

Everything? In her mind Alys felt anything but normal. She had not seen Ben outside the hospital since the evening he had said he loved her and asked her

how she'd like life as the wife of a G.P. He had been busy, of course. But she knew perfectly well that she had avoided even being alone in the theatre office or sitting room with him, or when she had, she had kept up a conversation about the work. It wasn't that she wanted to avoid Ben. She was very fond of him. Indeed she felt that if she could once get Richard out of her mind she could love Ben a great deal. The truth was, she felt that Ben was quietly waiting for her to make up her mind, to give him some sign. But she was balking at decision. She did not really want to put Richard out of her mind.

She heard Ben's voice as, the operation finished, no doubt, he went into the surgeons' changing room. She rose and went into the theatre kitchen to make some fresh tea for him. Having made it she took it into the sitting room where she knew he would come.

"Oh, so there you are, Alys," he said as he entered. "I thought you must be off duty."

She told him no, and poured out his tea. "I went for my tea and was delayed, then Matron sent for me," she explained.

"Trouble? Or a rise in salary?" he asked in fun.

"Neither, really," she told him. "It was about that business in the Home. It's all cleared up now. At least, the police have decided there's no case. We shan't be seeing any more of Detective-Sergeant Maxwell, thank goodness."

"Did they—or rather he—find out who the culprit was?"

"Well—yes, but I've been told not to tell. And I'd rather not, Ben."

"Fair enough. I understand. As long as you're in the clear—"

"Yes, Ben, I am."

She thought how much more faith Ben had shown

in her than Richard had. Richard had definitely taken Olivia's part in the other business. Did he know the truth about that? she wondered. She doubted it. Olivia still went about as though she was something special to him. At every opportunity she talked about where they had been, what they had been doing together.

"You don't look exactly overjoyed, though," Ben's voice broke into her thoughts.

Her unhappy reverie had shown in her face, obviously, and Ben had misinterpreted the cause.

"It's been an unpleasant business, Ben," she answered.

She went on to tell him that she would not be in theatre after Saturday.

"What time do you finish on Saturday?" he asked.

"Four-thirty."

"I have a weekend coming up. How about doing something on Saturday evening?"

It was inevitable. There was no escaping it. Alys pulled herself together. What was the use of pining after Richard?

"Yes, all right, Ben. Come to my place for tea. There's a film at the Odeon I'd like to see—if that's all right with you," she said a little jerkily.

"That will be fine, Alys. Thanks for the tea. I'd best be off now."

He sounded rather absentminded, which surprised her in a way. But she had no time to dwell on the thought. The telephone rang to tell her to have theatre ready immediately for an emergency peritonitis being sent in by the consultant in general surgery, the patient being a personal friend of his.

Swiftly, Alys went into action, her personal problems pushed into the background for the time being.

This patient's peritonitis was caused by a burst abscess on the appendix. He was a young man, lean and intelligent-looking, though his face when he was wheeled straight into the anaesthetic room from the receiving ward had that typical abdominal appearance —the *facies Hippocratica*, so called because the hollow cheeks, the drawn and anxious expression and the bright but sunken eyes was first described by Hippocrates.

The peritoneal cavity was drained and the appendix removed. The surgeon decided that a drainage tube was not necessary in this case and so the abdomen was closed in the usual way. By the time the operation was finished and theatre cleared up and made ready for anything else which might come along, it was time for the day staff to go off duty.

It was then that it suddenly occured to her that if Night Sister had no family, where would she go, if Matron had asked her to leave at a moment's notice? Had she friends? The thing worried her. If Sister had nowhere else to go she could stay at the flat for a while. After all, it would be easy to retrieve any articles Sister might take. The only thing was, would she wander to other parts of the house and pick things up? It would hardly be fair to Mrs. Wells to take Sister Halesworth there without consulting her. Yet how could she give Sister away like that? There was no need, of course, for her to wander over the rest of the house. The flat was entirely self-contained, and Sister Halesworth was no ordinary thief. She did not go *looking* for things to steal. The articles she had picked up in the Nurses' Home had been things she had seen on her rounds. So far as Alys could remember Mrs. Wells did not have knick-knacks in the hall. She did not even hang coats there.

Her thoughts brought her to the door of night Sister's room. After a momentary hesitation, Alys tapped on the door. She could at least have a chat with Sister.

"Who is it?" Night Sister called out.

When Alys called out her name, the door opened a little. "I'm busy, Sister. What is it you want?" she asked guardedly.

"I—just wondered if there was anything I could do for you." The door opened a fraction more, and Alys could see that Sister was packing. "Perhaps I could give you a hand with your luggage. I see you're going away."

The Sister's hand dropped from the door and she moved listlessly in a way which was a vague invitation to Alys to enter. Alys stepped inside and closed the door.

Silently, the night Sister went on with her packing. Obviously she did not want to talk about what had happened, even though it was likely that she was aware Alys knew all about it.

"Are you catching a train, Sister?" Alys asked, beginning to fold the pile of clothes which lay on the bed.

"No, I'm going to a hotel. I've hardly had time to make any arrangements."

"But didn't Matron suggest that you stayed here until you had?"

The other's thin face became even more drawn. "She did, but I wanted to get away. I told her I was staying the weekend with friends."

"I see. Have you somewhere in mind after that?"

"Yes. Someone I knew years ago. But I shan't be able to ring her until Monday morning. She's on the phone at work, but not at home."

"Have you booked a room at a hotel?" Alys asked her.

"Not yet," came the stiff-lipped reply.

Alys did not know the other very well, new as the Sister was to the hospital, but she had a strong feeling that the show of pride might be just a cover for sense of failure and uncertainty.

"I was wondering," Alys said, taking a sudden plunge, "whether you'd like to stay the weekend with me."

The other's movements halted abruptly, then slowly she turned and looked at Alys incredulously.

"Are you serious?"

Alys swallowed. "Of course."

The thin lips quivered. "You—you know all about me—yet you're willing to, you want me to—"

Alys nodded. "There's only one snag. I've got someone coming to tea and I've promised to go out this evening. If you're sure you don't mind being left in the flat on your own—"

She broke off. Sister Halesworth's lips had begun to tremble uncontrollably. Suddenly she sank down on the bed and covered her face with her hands. Her shoulders began to shake and a peculiar, high-pitched sound escaped her.

"I can't believe it. After all I've done. I never meant to take those things. Your cup and saucer, all the other things. If it hadn't been for Edna—but even she couldn't hide what she was doing for me. I don't know why I do it. It's like a nightmare, really it is!"

Alys put her arm around the thin shoulders. "I understand, Sister. Don't upset yourself. This is something you need help with. It's too big for you to cope with alone. Come along now, let's finish this packing and I'll go and bring my car round to the side entrance and we can load up."

Sister dried her eyes and stood up slowly. "I'll never forget this, Newton. Never."

"Nonsense, my dear," Alys said gently.

When the packing was all but completed she brought her car round and they carried the various suitcases to the lift and so out to the car. There was no heavy trunk, fortunately, and Sister's wardrobe was small. Her books were few, and these had been placed at the bottom of one of her suitcases.

Alys drove to the flat as quickly as she could, hoping that Ben would not be there before her. She told Sister who it was she was expecting.

"You can please yourself, my dear, whether you have tea in your own room or with us."

"Does he know about me?" the other asked in a small voice.

"Certainly not."

But Sister said she had a headache, and decided to stay in her room, after all. Ben arrived just as Alys was preparing tea. He kissed her and thrust an enormous bouquet into her arms.

"From me to you, with love," he said with a smile.

"Ben, how lovely!"

She filled a pail full of water and stood the flowers in it, then continued to prepare tea. Ben watched her.

"Who's the tray for?" he asked as she placed a small tea pot alongside the other items.

She told him, also that Sister Halesworth was staying the weekend and wanted to be quiet for a while. To her relief Ben made no comment. Perhaps he guessed the truth, knowing what she had confided in him a little while ago, and understood sufficiently to ask no more questions.

Sister insisted on Alys leaving the washing up for her to do. "You run along and enjoy yourself—and don't worry about me—Alys, your name is, isn't it? I shan't budge from the flat."

Alys could have wept at this. "You're one up on me. I don't know what your Christian name is."

"It's Charlotte—for my sins. But what few friends I have call me Lottie."

Of course, that's what Nurse Farrel had called her, Alys recalled.

"Well, try and enjoy the evening, Lottie," she said. "Switch television on, help yourself to what's in the fridge for supper. You'll find some ham and cheese, eggs and tomatoes and so on. 'Bye for now."

"Ready, then?" asked Ben when she joined him again.

She nodded absently. She had a feeling something was going to happen tonight. There was something in the air, in Ben's attitude. Was he going to talk about marriage, press her to a definite decision? But the way she was feeling at the present moment, uneasy and at odds with herself, she was sure she wouldn't be able to give him one.

"A penny for them," Ben said as he drove in the direction of town.

She started guiltily. "Oh—sorry, Ben. I was day-dreaming, I suppose."

Ben flicked a glance at her and patted her knee sympathetically. Her face obviously gave more away than her words.

"I know," he said. "You've had a very worrying time lately. But it's behind you now, I imagine. At least—"

He broke off as a car in front stopped suddenly. Alys did not ask him what he had been going to say, and he appeared to forget. They reached the cinema they were going to and Ben found a space in which to park his car.

Alys was glad to relax in the near-darkness. At first, as the news and the second feature was shown, her mind kept letting in little bits of her problems. Richard, Ben, Lottie and her troubles, and all that had happened during the last few weeks. But at last, when the main film came on, she was able to forget things for a while. It was a good film—and like most good films contained a love story. Two people in love, and after many difficulties, in which pride paid a large part, all ended happily. But real life wasn't always like that, she found herself thinking.

When they came out Ben suggested supper, and so they went straight into the cinema restaurant. When he had given their order Ben said, smiling at her across the table :

"Enjoy the film?"

She nodded, but gave a rueful smile. "I wonder how often everything turns out happily as it did for those two characters? There was a time when you couldn't see how it possibly could."

Ben eyed her thoughtfully. "It was a great story, of course, but all fiction is a little removed from life, isn't it? Real life is never quite so difficult—at least, not for the majority, and never quite as idealistic. It's somewhere between the two. For most people life is pretty uneventful in comparison. Love isn't always the dramatic thing set out in some books and films, either. For most people it's something that grows out of a mutual liking, and it's often stronger, in the end, than the other kind."

She smiled a little. "You make it sound so simple and uncomplicated, Ben. But, you know, it does often happen in real life that love is one-sided."

"No one knows that better than I do," Ben answered. "But believe me, Alys, a love that isn't returned dies a natural death. It's bound to sooner or later."

"I suppose so," she admitted, fighting down a sickening despair.

The waiter brought the first course of their meal, and for a little while they ate in silence. It was Ben who spoke first.

"I don't suppose you've seen much of Richard lately, have you? He's still seeing Olivia, as I suppose you know."

Alys took a deep breath. "I had heard—and no, I've

seen nothing at all of him outside the hospital since—
oh, for quite a time, really."

"I thought not. I don't know about you, Alys, but I
still feel I'd like to get away from hospital life. I don't
mean away from surgery, in particular, but I would
like my own practice, a real home of my own, wouldn't
you?"

"I have my flat now," she murmured.

"True, but is that enough? Don't get the idea that
what I've just said is *all* I want. It isn't. Alys, you said
not long ago that the idea of being the wife of a G.P.—
my wife—sounded very attractive to you. Does it still?
Because, if so—well, this may not be the ideal time to
ask you. I mean, there's no moonlight and roses, but
I'm asking you seriously if you'll marry me, Alys."

Alys put down her spoon. In spite of half expecting
this she still had not a straight answer ready.

"Ben, that's—nice of you. Do you—want me to say
yes or no now—tonight?"

He lowered his spoon, too, and the waiter came to
take their plates.

"Is it such a difficult decision, Alys? You know how
I feel about you, and—I'd hoped—"

"Yes, Ben, I know. And you're so right about many
of the things you've said. Love isn't always the stupend-
ous thing of the films."

He was right, too, about love that wasn't returned.
She couldn't hang on to her love for Richard for ever.
And what she felt for Ben could deepen. And yet—

The waiter came with their second course and Alys
happened to glance across the room. The next moment
she stifled a swift intake of breath. Just entering the
restaurant was Richard. With him was Olivia.

As Alys watched them make their way to an empty
table all indecision about marrying Ben vanished.

CHAPTER TEN

BEN saw the change of expression on Alys's face, and followed her gaze.

"Well, well. Talk of the devil!"

Alys eyed the food on her plate without interest but picked up her knife and fork. Ben looked at her, but said nothing for a moment, but after a while he prompted quietly:

"You were saying, Alys?"

"What I was saying isn't really important now, Ben," she said in a low voice. "The answer to your question, I'm afraid, has to be—no. I—hope you don't mind too much."

Ben's disappointment showed in his face, then his jaw tightened.

"If that's your answer, I'll just have to take it. I'm sorry, of course. But—"

"Ben, it wouldn't have been right," she said quickly, feeling desperately sorry as his shoulders slumped a little. He had been let down by Olivia, now she herself had disappointed him. But one did not marry for pity. "You—you must believe in love, my dear, and believe that one day you'll meet a woman who'll really love you—and you her."

He breathed heavily and shook his head. "I've told you, I do love you."

Alys held his gaze across the table. "I think you're fond of me, as I am of you. But I don't think you're passionately *in love* with me. And I believe that two people have to start off marriage with that all-consuming passion for each other. I—I'm not saying it can't grow, that there's no room left for growth. It—it does so in a different way, that's all."

"How can you know, Alys?" he asked heavily. "That's just how you'd like it to be. You're an idealist. That passion you talk about. It doesn't last. It's like the bubbles in champagne."

Now it was her turn to shake her head. "I'm sorry, Ben, but I can't agree with you. The kind of passion I mean is a passion of intensity, of *feeling*, of love for a person, a—a belief that without that person life has no meaning, that you simply cannot live without him—"

Her voice broke suddenly. This was the way she felt about Richard, while he—she struggled to regain her composure.

"Oh, Alys, Alys! Can't you see the hopelessness if your love isn't returned? How can you continue to feel as you do under those circumstances?"

With a great effort Alys took command of herself. "I'm sorry, Ben, but while I do feel this way, I simply can't even consider marrying anyone else."

Seeing Richard unexpectedly like this—even in the company of Olivia—had suddenly brought this truth home to her, had made her realise afresh just how much she still loved Richard. She felt convinced, too, that Ben was not really in love with her. She could understand his longing for a wife and a home of his own. That feeling was not by any means confined to women. And she felt he certainly had affection for her. But she wanted to be loved in the same way that she loved Richard. Whether she would feel about him for the rest of her life as she did now, particularly if he married someone else, was doubtful, she supposed, though at the present moment she was convinced that she would never love anyone else. But while she did feel this way, it would be neither right nor fair to promise to marry anyone, not even Ben.

"Ben, you do see, don't you?" she appealed.

He gave a brief smile. "I see that your answer is no, at any rate."

They made some pretence of carrying on with their meal. Alys deliberately refrained from looking round to see where Richard and Olivia were sitting. Whether she and Ben had been seen by them she had no way of knowing.

"What will you do, Ben?" she asked in a little while. "Will you stay on at the hospital or look around for something else?"

Ben sighed. "I really don't know. I'll have to think about it some more. I think perhaps a fresh start somewhere else might be a good idea."

She nodded. "As a matter of fact, Ben, I think I might do the same. I'm back in the Home tomorrow, as you know, and Richard is panel doctor to most of the nurses. We—do little else but fight each time we meet, and I don't think I can stand much more of it."

Ben reached out and touched her hand in sympathy. "I know how you feel. At the risk of repeating myself, may I say, my dear, that it won't last. You'll get over it quicker, though, by getting away." He laughed shortly. "It's odd, isn't it—our comforting each other in this way? Not the way I planned things at all."

"Things *don't* always go as planned, Ben, do they? That's life, I guess."

"I suppose so," he said gloomily. Then suddenly he smiled. "Well, I must take your answer with as much grace as I can muster. Can I hope that we'll still be friends?"

"Ben, of course. I should be very miserable indeed if I thought I'd lost your friendship."

"Then let's drink to that, shall we?"

He called over the waiter and ordered a bottle of champagne, which Alys laughingly persuaded him to reduce to half a bottle, saying she really ought to get back to the flat and her guest sober.

Alys was relieved that Ben was taking her refusal so well. Even though—as she felt—he wasn't very deeply in love with her, he could well have been suffering from hurt pride or have displayed annoyance. She supposed Richard and Olivia were still in the restaurant as she had not seen them depart. She refrained from asking Ben.

Then all at once a voice asked silkily: "Celebrating something?"

Alys started and looked up to see Olivia beside her. Richard, a few paces away, nodded and was for continuing on his way.

It was Ben who answered. "Yes, we are," he said. "Sorry I can't ask you to join us. I'm afraid the bottle's all but empty."

Olivia laughed. "Don't worry. We're just going, anyway. Come along, Richard," she said, as though she were waiting for him, instead of the other way round. "Let's leave these two lovebirds to their little celebration."

She took Richard's arm and they continued on their way to the exit.

"Obviously, they think we're celebrating our engagement," Ben said ruefully. "They'll soon be put right, I daresay."

Alys didn't want to say that she hoped so. "I think if you don't mind, Ben, I ought to go now. I don't want to be late on account of Sister Halesworth."

Ben saw her to the front door of the house, then said goodnight, saying he wouldn't come up, seeing she had a guest.

He put a hand on Alys's shoulder. "You're a great girl, Alys. You've been very sweet to Sister. He'll be a very lucky man who marries you. Sorry it couldn't be me."

He didn't make any attempt to kiss her. With a smile and a wave he slipped back into the driving seat of his car, then drove off. With a weary little sigh, Alys climbed the stairs.

Lottie was in her room. Alys tapped on her door and entered when the other woman called out.

"Hope you don't mind. I brought a supper tray to bed," Lottie said, putting down her book. "I thought you might be bringing Mr. Chalmers up and I didn't want to be in the way."

"You wouldn't have been in the way," Alys assured her. "He didn't come up, anyway. Hope you haven't been bored on your own."

Lottie laughed shortly. "Heavens, no. I'm used to being alone. I watched television for a while until it palled, then made myself a ham sandwich." She paused, then asked: "Is—er—the house surgeon a particular friend of yours?"

"Sort of."

"Any possibility of marriage?"

Alys shook her head. "As a matter of fact, he did ask me this evening, but—"

"You said no?" Lottie gave her a keen look. "You and Kent were a bit friendly at one time, weren't you?"

Alys affected derision and amusement. "Friendly! We used to fight every other time we met."

Lottie smiled. "Ah, but they were friendly fights, weren't they? You know, he's more of a real man in many ways than Chalmers. For my taste, anyway, and I think for yours, too, eh? Isn't it him you're really set on?"

Alys did not answer at once. Sister was pretty shrewd. What was the point in denying it? The night Sister wouldn't be going back to the hospital, so wouldn't be able to give her away, even if she felt inclined to. Alys gave a small gesture of hopelessness.

"You've put your finger right on the spot, I'm afraid,

but it's only on my side, not on his. Still, I'll get over it in time, I expect. I'm sure I'm not the first to suffer from unrequited love by a long way."

She tried to sound lighthearted about it, but doubted if she deceived Sister.

"You talk as though it's hopeless," Lottie said. "How do you know that? He might be secretly in love with you, who knows?"

Alys shook her head. "Then why keep it a secret? He's had plenty of opportunity of letting me know. With a woman it's different, even in our modern times. At least, it is with me. I still want the man to do the chasing. If he showed any sign, of course, I'd meet him halfway. But—well, you know, a girl has her pride and all that."

"Yes," agreed Lottie.

Alys went to the door. "Well, I'm going to have my bath, then make a nightcap. Would you like another drink?"

But Lottie shook her head. "No, thanks. I think I'll put my light out and get some sleep."

And so Alys took away the supper tray and closed the door behind her. She deliberately did not dwell on the evening or think about Richard. But she did not need to actively think of Richard. He was always there, in her mind, a part of herself. And she knew perfectly well that he always would be.

Alys was due back on duty at one o'clock the following day. After a combination of breakfast and lunch she left Lottie in the flat and drove to the hospital, reporting first to Matron after pulling on her uniform cap.

"You'll do an evening round of the wards, Sister, will you?" asked Matron. "And I'm afraid you have a nurse in sick bay. It's Nurse Johns. She only came back from holiday last night, crawled on duty without breakfast and passed out in the middle of the morning. Dr. Kent was out, so one of the other M.O.s had a look at her. It sounds to me like a bilious attack."

"Her holiday wouldn't appear to have done her much good," Alys commented.

"No, but I expect the change has. Unless, of course, she's picked up some foreign germ or has a mild form of food poisoning. She went abroad with her parents. Apart from that there's been no change in the hospital since last night, and you can read the night report for yourself."

Matron went off to lunch, and Alys ran her eye down the night report. There had been no major operations on Saturday, as well she knew, and no emergencies after she had gone off duty. Friday's cases were, in the main, out of danger, and on the medical wards there was nothing that any staff nurse could not cope with. It looked like an unusually quiet weekend. She went over to sick bay.

"Well Nurse Johns, this is a fine howdy-do after your holiday. How do you feel now?"

"Awfully sick, Sister, and I keep going to the toilet. Apart from that—well, I do feel better in bed."

Alys smiled. "That goes without saying, Nurse. Have you been sick?"

"No, Sister."

"Let me look at your tongue." The girl opened her mouth and showed a heavily furred, almost green one. "Heavens, child, that's ghastly! You *must* be feeling ill. I suppose you've had nothing to eat today?"

"No, Sister, only a glass of milk at half past nine, and I wished I hadn't had it. I felt awfully sick afterwards."

"Hm. Obviously, your stomach needs a rest. Tell me about your holiday. Where did you go and what kind of food did you have?"

The girl had been to Italy in her father's car. By

air across the Channel, then from Ostend through Belgium, Germany and Austria by road.

"Were you sick on the journey?"

"No, Sister, I was fine—and we drove all night. My father and brother took it in turn. I expect I'd have been all right on the return journey, but this sickness came on the day before we set off back."

"And what made you sick then? Too much to eat and drink?"

This was denied vigorously. "I didn't have any more than anyone else. In fact, not as much as my brother. He ate loads and loads of strawberry cake and cream, and he drank more wine than I did, too."

"Maybe your brother's inside is stronger than yours. Some can take it, others can't. You can't judge one person by another when it comes to stomachs. Anyway, we'll see what Dr. Kent says when he comes. Meanwhile, just rest, and I'll get you a mouthwash. Have you got much pain?"

A frown creased the nurse's forehead. "Well, it's not *bad,* Sister. It just comes and goes."

Half an hour later Richard rang the Nurses' Home. "Is that Sister Newton?" he enquired as she lifted the receiver. "Kent here. I just rang to make sure someone was there when I come to see the nurse who's in sick bay."

Kent. It had been a long time since he had called himself that to her.

"Yes, I'm here, Doctor," she answered, feeling her heart sick within her. "What time are you coming?"

"Right away," he said, and rang off in the middle of her "Very well, Doctor."

Feeling utterly wretched, she went along to sick bay to await his arrival. Even his sarcasm was preferrable to this strict formality. She braced herself to match his attitude with her own formality.

He greeted her with a cool nod. "Good afternoon, Sister. Now, Nurse, what seems to be the trouble?"

Haltingly Nurse Johns told him her symptoms.

"I see." He glanced at the temperature and pulse chart Alys held out for him to see. "And what have you been eating?"

"Nothing, Doctor."

Alys intervened to explain that Nurse had been abroad and had been ill just before setting out for home, also on the return journey, upon which he quipped the girl about consuming too much Italian food and wine. He looked at her tongue and examined her abdomen and asked about the nature of her pain.

"You say you began to feel ill after you'd been in Italy for about a week?" he asked when he had finished.

"Yes, Doctor."

"Is it your first time abroad? Your parents, too?"

"My father has travelled, but not my mother. It was her first time. We didn't drink any of their water—except in tea or coffee. We thought it was all right so long as it had been boiled."

Richard smiled and shook his head. "Don't take it for granted that everybody's water except our own is impure. It isn't. No, Nurse, it isn't so much the water. At least, it's not that it's impure, it's just different from ours. The real culprit is the food. You see, there are a certain amount of germs in all the food we eat, even at home. There are bound to be. Not everything is sterile, is it? But you see, at home, your system has developed anti-bodies to fight these germs. When you go to places like Italy you don't have time to develop fresh antibodies, so you become a victim to infections that don't bother the Italians. They've developed their own immunity, just as you do at home."

"But why was I the only one to get upset?"

He smiled. "Hardly fair, is it? Why does one person catch colds and another not? Some have less resistance than others. Perhaps you're one of them. You've got to face the fact and take necessary precautions. Or better still, take more vitamins. Now, let's get down to treatment. Some tablets, medicine and special diet. The lot." Alys handed him the treatment card, and he scribbled down the prescriptions. "Oh—and stay in bed, young lady," he added.

No wonder he was so popular with the nurses. And no wonder she loved him. He had sympathy, a sense of humour, understanding, intelligence. She could go on listing his virtues. If only he loved her as she loved him —or even half as much. But this was foolish thinking.

She glanced down at the card. He had ordered one of the drugs containing the active ingredients telescoped as Iodochlorhydroxyquinoline which could be bought at any chemist for the prevention and treatment of intestinal infections, along with *Mist. Kaolin et opii.*

"No point in giving her an antibiotic," he said. "No specific organism is responsible for her condition, I feel sure. All the same, keep an eye on her, and I'll come and see her again tomorrow."

As he spoke he had progressed out of the room and was walking along the corridor towards the stairs. At the top he paused before going down to the ground floor.

"There's no need for you to come any further, Sister. I can find my own way out—I think."

Before she could even answer he was flinging himself down the stairs. Alys felt tears prick her eyes. This was even worse than before. She couldn't stand it. She really couldn't. She must get away from here. Must leave.

Straight away she went over to the dispensary. She simply dared not allow herself to seek the privacy of her office or sitting room. If she did she knew she would be unable to hold back the tears which felt as if they were filling her throat and sinuses to bursting point. Then, having obtained the medicine and tablets, she returned to the sick room and administered them and made the nurse as comfortable as she could.

"Would you like a portable radio or a book?" she asked. "I'd really advise a book. Reading might send you off to sleep, and you could do with all the rest you can get."

By the time she had done all she could for her patient it was afternoon tea time, and not wanting to be alone, Alys went along to the Sisters' sitting room where tea was served. But afterwards she wished she hadn't. She hadn't reckoned on Olivia passing on what she thought was the news of her engagement to Ben. Almost immediately she was pounced on by two of the ward Sisters. Romance, still more an actual engagement, was always a subject for gossip.

"What's this about you and Ben Chalmers? When's the wedding, then?"

"We're not engaged," Alys told them firmly.

"Eh? Oh, come off it, Newton. Champagne to celebrate and all that. Who do you think you're kidding?"

"If you want to keep it quiet, I'm afraid you've got another think coming," the other one said. "The cat, dear Home Sister, is well and truly out of the bag."

Alys sighed. "It doesn't follow that because two people—notably one man and one woman—drink champagne that they're engaged."

"No, but one doesn't drink champagne every day of one's life. If you weren't celebrating your engagement, what were you celebrating. Eternal friendship?"

"As a matter of fact, yes, that's just what we were celebrating."

She didn't want to go into details, to tell them that Ben had asked her and she had said no. It would then be passed from lip to lip that she had "turned him down," and that wouldn't be very nice for Ben.

But obviously her denial had not convinced the two young Sisters. They were not going to be done out of their romance.

"Well, that's one way of putting it," she was told. "It's nice if you can remain friends after you're married, I'm sure. If you can't have eternal love—"

"Oh, for goodness' sake—" implored Alys. "Why on earth should we want to keep it secret?"

"Why indeed? I expect you have your reasons, but you know what it's like in hospital. Once a thing is out—"

Alys gave up. What was the use? This sort of thing had happened before. Rumours of engagements which petered out after a while, and of course the other way round. Two people, not wanting their affair talked about, had surprised everybody—or nearly everybody— by suddenly announcing that they were married. If she and Ben both continued to deny it—because, of course, the rumour would soon reach the medical staff, even if it had not done so already—then it would die in time.

In one sense she was beyond caring very much. She went about that day feeling as though her heart was quietly breaking. If only Richard would even begin teasing her again. Anything would be preferable to his politeness.

Her nurse-patient became a little better during the evening. Alys set off to do Matron's evening round of the wards, in most cases merely picking up the summaries of the reports and enquiring as to whether there was any change. But on one of Richard's wards where the Sister was off duty she found the staff nurse at the bedside of a patient who had suddenly become unconscious. He had been admitted about a week ago with a severe myocardial infection and was being treated with bed rest. The staff nurse was giving him oxygen by B.L.B. mask, but the man's pulse was impalpable and his respirations gasping.

"Send for Dr. Kent, Nurse," Alys told her. "I'll massage his heart."

The staff nurse dashed to the telephone and Alys began the massage. At the present moment the patient was in the semi-recumbent position on a backrest, and this acted as a firm base. Alys kept up the massage until Richard came, but the patient was still gasping.

"Take away the backrest, Nurse," ordered Richard, "and lay him flat. Then I'll take over the massage, Sister."

But it was in vain, and Alys began to fear the patient might die. Richard must have had the same feeling. For a second his eyes met those of Alys.

"The emergency tray and defibrillator?" she asked quickly.

"Yes—and the Boyles—quickly!"

She sent the staff nurse to the theatre for the defibrillator and the Boyles respirator and brought the emergency tray. The next hour was a desperate fight for the man's life. His heart sounds became inaudible and respirations ceased. Swiftly, Richard opened up the man's chest and internal massage began. The ventricles then began to fibrillate, so an endotracheal tube was inserted and mouth-to-tube respiration started. Ten minutes later gasping respiration had returned, and Alys felt she had started to breathe again, too. She saw the beads of perspiration standing out on Richard's brow as he connected the patient to the Boyles machine.

After this, and with the arrival of the resident anaesthetist, the defibrillator was used three times, and a hundred volts applied for just over a tenth of a second. With each shock the patient went into opisthotonous, and at last normal rhythm was restored. The chest wound edges were brought together by strong forceps, and his blood pressure and the tracing by the electro-cardiograph showed sinus rhythm with ventricular ectopic beats.

Richard indulged in a deep breath. "Theatre now then, Sister."

A stretcher was brought and Alys went to the theatre with the patient herself. Here, a tube drain was inserted into the thorax through a stab incision and connected to an underwater seal, then the wound was sutured.

"Are you taking him back to the ward yourself, Sister?" asked Richard. Alys said she was. "He'll need to be specialled," he told her. "He'll probably become restless, anyway. Sunday is a damned awkward day for staff, I know, but he mustn't be left for a minute. Are you in charge of the hospital at the moment? If so, see what you can do, will you?"

"Yes, of course."

"Good. I'll be along shortly to have a look at him."

Alys saw the unconscious patient back in his bed. "I expect you're way behind with the rest of your treatment, aren't you?" she said to the staff nurse. "And goodness knows where I'm going to find a special. Will you stay with him yourself for a while, and I'll finish my round and see who can be spared. I may have to special him myself until the night staff come on duty. Or even after that."

The staff on all the wards was at the very minimum, but help as well as a special must be found from some-where. For an hour or more work on that ward had vir-ually ceased, all attention being rightly focused on saving the life of the one patient, either at the bedside or in fetching and carrying.

Alys finished her round quickly, then sent a junior nurse from a ward which appeared to be well forward with its work. She went to stay with the patient herself, leaving a note for the night Sister that a night special was needed.

The man was restless, as Richard had foreseen. Alys gave him the intramuscular injection of phenobarbitone Richard had ordered, and intermittently administered oxygen. He also perspired profusely, and so Alys sponged him. She had just finished when Richard appeared. He looked surprised to see her still there.

"Nice work, Sister," he said quietly, looking down at his patient.

Alys could not answer. Ridiculously, her heart swelled with pride at his praise, and the gentle tone of his voice tore at her heart.

He looked at the temperature chart and the blood pressure reading and felt the pulse for himself. The beat was irregular, Alys knew, and could not be felt at all in the right arm.

"We're lucky it can be felt anywhere," he murmured.

"Yes, indeed."

Richard picked up the treatment card. "I'll write him up for a quarter of morphia. He's bound to have some pain during the night. I shall be doing another round later, of course, but I want to know the minute he becomes conscious."

"Yes, Doctor."

He looked at her. "Couldn't you find a special?"

"Only a junior," she told him. "And the nurses needed help on the ward. I've left word for the night Sister. She'll send someone along."

He inclined his head, but said no more, and went away again. But the night Sister was a long time sending a special, and Alys hung on so that the ward night nurse and her junior could settle the rest of the patients for the night. As a consequence she was still at the bedside when Richard came once more.

"Good lord! You still here, Alys?"

Her heart leapt at his use of her Christian name. It could have been a slip of the tongue, of course, she told herself swiftly.

"Only until the ward nurse is ready to take over. Then I shall go and find out who Night Sister is sending."

"I should very much like to know that myself—and when," Richard muttered. "You should have been at home ages ago."

For a minute or two he then directed his attention to the patient. The drainage and underwater seal were satisfactory and there was no evidence of lung injury, but he was developing surgical emphysema.

"Hm. We'll have to watch that. As soon as he's conscious I want him gradually sat up. Where the hell is that night special? I'm going to find out myself and—"

There was a movement at the ward door. Alys glanced in that direction to see the night Sister, accompanied by a student nurse.

"Richard, please don't say anything. I've been quite happy to stay on for a while."

His dark eyes looked swiftly into hers and held them for a moment. Like a smouldering fire that suddenly bursts into flame Alys felt her love for him leap to the surface spontaneously. In a panic she looked away.

"I'll leave you to pass on your instructions to the special, Doctor," she said swiftly.

"No, don't go. Wait for me. There's something I want to say to you."

"Very well."

She had to do as he asked, not knowing whether it was something to do with a patient he wanted to speak to her about. She waited in the ward corridor, and after a moment or two he joined her. She tried not to look at him, afraid that her love for him might show.

"I want to thank you for what you've done," he said. "I simply don't know what I'd have done without you."

She pulled the drawstring of her defences swiftly. "I don't need any thanks. I only did my job, and I was very, very glad indeed to have been able to help."

She began to walk towards the main corridor, and he fell into step beside her. At the end of the ward corridor Alys paused.

"Well, goodnight, Doctor."

There was a pause. "You've got your car outside, I expect," said Richard then.

"Yes, thank you." Her longing for physical contact, the touch of his hand, the feel of his arms, a desire to run her fingers gently down his cheek was unbearable. With a swiftly murmured "Goodnight," she hurried to the nearest exit and her car. She let in the clutch, struggling to keep back her tears, and only by concentrating fiercely on her driving did she succeed.

Alys scarcely knew whether to be glad or sorry about the presence of Lottie in the flat. But in the end she was glad. When Lottie remarked on her lateness, Alys told her all about the emergency over the coffee and sandwiches that the other woman had prepared.

"I'm going to miss you, Lottie, when you've gone," she said just before they said goodnight. "It's nice having someone to talk to at the end of the day."

Lottie smiled. "You're not used to being alone, that's easy to see. And I should think that when you're in love you feel loneliness even more. Why don't you get someone to share this flat with you?"

"It's worth a thought. When I first came here it seemed as if Mrs. Wells and I might become friends, but I don't see as much of her as I expected to." Alys then asked Lottie about her plans for the following day. "Will you travel to your friend's place tomorrow, if she can have you?"

"I think so, yes. Probably in the afternoon. What time are you off duty tomorrow?"

"Evening," Alys told her. "You know, you're quite welcome to stay on here for a while, if you'd like to."

Lottie shook her head. "That's very, very nice of you, my dear, and I appreciate your kindness more than it's possible for me to say. In fact, I shall never forget what you did for me. But I think it best for me to depart just as soon as I'm able. I—just couldn't trust myself not to do something to—"

Alys knew what she meant, and protested, but Lottie shook her head.

"No, no. Some day, perhaps, if we're still in touch, but not just now. I'll say goodbye to you either tonight or in the morning, and if I do catch a train before you come home, I'll give you a ring."

But Lottie was still fast asleep when Alys softly tapped on her door the next morning and opened it. Wishing her guest a silent farewell Alys went out again, closing the door behind her.

It was a pleasant change to be in the Nurses' Home once more and at her job without the presence of Detective Sergeant Maxwell. Going first to the sick bay, she was pleased to find her patient much improved. At about eleven o'clock Richard paid his visit. He looked worn out, and Alys wondered just how much sleep he had had last night. She asked him how his patient was.

"Conscious," he told her. "He even spoke to me this morning, for which heaven be thanked."

Alys agreed that it was indeed a miracle. "How's the emphysema?" she asked.

"Pretty severe now. I've ordered a chest X-ray and put him on penicillin and streptomycin and cortisone therapy."

"And cardiac drugs?" She felt she must go on talking.

"Procainamide," he said absently.

They entered the sick bay and found Nurse Johns reading a nursing textbook.

"My goodness, you must be feeling better!" laughed Richard.

"I sit my prelim in October," Nurse Johns said, laying the book face downwards on the bed, "and I feel I don't know a thing."

"Well, you should know about gastro-enteritis now, anyway. How do you feel?" He nodded as the nurse told him she was much better and that her symptoms had all but gone. "That's good, but these kind of things have a habit of lingering, you know, and of recurring at the slightest indiscretion in eating for quite a while. Stay in bed today and rest and then you get up tomorrow. But stay off duty and on your diet for another few days at least." He smiled. "I don't think we can give you any sick leave, as you've just had your holiday. At least, not without bringing down the wrath of Matron on my head."

And this time he allowed Alys to see him to the door of the Home, but without speaking one word except the usual, "Thank you, Sister."

Shortly after lunch Lottie rang her. "My friend can have me, Alys," she said, "and there's a train at two-thirty. I've ordered a taxi and I'm just about ready to go."

Strangely, Alys had a feeling of regret. "I wish you could have stayed, Lottie. Take care of yourself, won't you? And do let me know how you get on."

"I will," Lottie answered, and once more thanked her for everything.

The next time Alys saw Nurse Farrel she told her of the ex-night Sister's plans, and how she had spent the weekend at the flat.

"Oh, Sister, I'm sure that helped a lot. I don't

suppose she'll write to me, but I would like to know when you hear from her again."

"If I hear," Alys said with a slight smile.

"If Lottie—I mean Sister—said she was going to write, then she will," declared Nurse Farrel.

During the afternoon Ben telephoned. "The hospital have got us engaged," he said. "Did you know? Or need I ask?"

"You needn't ask. I hope it's not bothering you, Ben. I expect it's Olivia who's started it. But the rumour will soon die down."

"It's not bothering me to any extent—except that I still wish it were true. I really rang up to tell you that I resigned this morning."

"Oh, Ben! Have you something in view?"

"No. I made up my mind all at once. I shall take a holiday while I look around and answer a few ads. By the way, Alys, if you should ever change your mind about me, you will let me know, won't you? I'll give you an address before I leave."

She was touched, but she felt certain that once away from the hospital he would gradually forget her.

"Ben, that's good of you. But I'm sure one of these days you'll be writing to tell me you really are engaged."

"I doubt it. We'll have an evening out somewhere before I go, anyway, eh?"

"Of course."

She was tempted to stay out of the Sisters' sitting room, but decided it would be silly, really. When she did go in for tea it was to find that already the news of Ben's resignation was being discussed. Immediately, of course, this was connected with Alys, and she was plied with questions about his plans. Olivia was in the room and took very little part in the conversation until someone suddenly said to her:

"What about you and Kent, Longford? Hasn't he popped the question yet?"

Olivia raised her eyebrows superciliously. "He doesn't have to pop the question in so many words. But when we *do* go out to celebrate it won't be in any two-bit restaurant where Ben Chalmers took Newton. Richard and I only went in there because we happened to have been to see the film in the building."

"That's the only reason Ben and I went in, too," Alys told her in a strained voice, and got up and left the room.

So Richard's friendship with Olivia had progressed as far as that? They had "an understanding." This served to put the seal on the hopelessness of her loving him as nothing else could have done. He was as good as engaged to Olivia. The finality of it was like a door shut for ever in her face, leaving her lost and desolated.

Later, as she was driving home, she thought of Ben. How tempting to ring him, to tell him she would go with him, after all. Stay here she simply could not, if Richard were to remain.

She put her car away and climbed the stairs listlessly. At the top she suddenly remembered that she had left her key with Lottie in case she wanted to go out. Where had Lottie left it? She bent down and looked under the doormat, but it wasn't there. How on earth was she going to get in, and what had Lottie done with the key? Automatically, she tried the knob and to her surprise the door opened. Moreover the light was on.

"Lottie!" she called out. "Are you there? Didn't you go, after all? Or did you miss your train or something?"

She advanced into the room, then suddenly she stood quite still, unable to believe what she saw.

"Richard! What on earth are you doing here?"

CHAPTER ELEVEN

HE grinned up at her from the depths of one of her armchairs.

"Hello, Alys. Are you pleased to see me, or are you going to send me away?"

She felt bewildered, not sure how to take him. "How —did you get in? Was the key under the mat?"

He shook his head. "Er—Lottie, as you call her, gave it to me."

"But why? I don't understand. And when did you see her?"

"This afternoon at the station. She was in quite a fluster. She had forgotten to leave the key behind."

"I see."

He gazed up at her. "I wonder if you do?" Then with a sudden apology for his bad manners he rose to his feet. "Look, you must be tired. Why don't you sit down and let me make you some tea? Or maybe you'd like to get out of your uniform. I won't stay long, if you don't want me to, but there are one or two things I want to tell you before I do go."

She was too confused to argue. She moved in the direction of her room and he went into the kitchen as if he knew the way blindfold. What were the "one or two things" he wanted to tell her? Had he found out the truth about the missing earrings and all the other things and wanted to offer an apology for believing her guilty, or at least, having some suspicion of her? It was too bad of Lottie to forget to leave the key behind like that.

Foolishly, perhaps, she searched her wardrobe for

the kind of dress she thought Richard would like and which suited her. This was ridiculous, of course, she told herself, and reached for a skirt and top. But the temptation to look attractive for him was too great. She chose one she had only worn a few times, a deceptively simple shirtwaister with a trim bodice and a softly flowing skirt, its rich colour and unusual design looking well on her.

She removed her old make-up with cleansing cream and applied fresh, then ran a comb through her hair, eyeing herself in the mirror almost angrily, and feeling that for two pins she would take it all off again. He would think she had dressed up for his benefit. Why hadn't she just put on something old? Then his voice called out:

"It's made. What are you doing in there, for goodness' sake?"

Really! "What do you think I'm doing?" she retorted, emerging from her room. "Having got out of my uniform I had to get into something else, didn't I?"

She saw his lips twitch with amusement as he set out the cups and saucers.

"Well, I suppose so," he said, then turned to look at her. She had the satisfaction of seeing the frank admiration in his eyes. "I say! Well worth it, anyhow. Do sit down, madam, and I'll pour your tea."

She did as he said, and watched him, smiling faintly, as he placed a small table at her hand and her cup of tea upon it.

"Anything to eat?"

"No, thanks."

"A cigarette?"

She shook her head. All she wanted to do was let her gaze rest on his profile, his dark hair, his form, to indulge in the wonderful feeling of peace and happiness in his presence. If only this could last for ever. If only—

Afraid that he might guess her thoughts, she sipped

her tea for a minute, then without looking at him at all, she made herself ask :

"What did you want to talk about, Richard?"

He smiled a little from the chair opposite. "Don't rush me, Alys. There's rather a lot of it, and I'm not sure where to begin."

He put his cup down and leaned his head on the back of his chair, his gaze directed across the room thoughtfully.

She moved restlessly in her chair and said in a tight voice : "If—if it's about that business of Olivia's earrings, it doesn't really matter. It was a misunderstanding, that's all, and I can quite understand your taking her part and thinking the worst of me."

He frowned as if he hadn't heard her properly, and his gaze swivelled back to her.

"What? What did you say? Olivia's earrings? Darling, what on earth are you talking about?"

She flushed at the term of endearment and compressed her lips tightly.

"Richard, *please*—"

His eyes wide, he rose slowly from his chair and came towards her. Then, one hand on each arm of her chair, he bent over her, his lips curved into a teasing smile. A smile she had seen on his lips so often.

"I think, my dear little, my very reverend Home Sister, I'd better come straight to the point and make my explanations later. The plain truth is, I'm in love with you. Madly, passionately, frustratingly in love with you."

My very reverend Home Sister. She stared at him, pain and anger tearing at her heart. She pushed him away from her.

"For heaven's sake, I'm tired of that old joke, and this time you've gone too far. Do you mind leaving, please, Richard?"

He straightened up and half turned. Alys leaned her head against the backrest of her chair and prayed that she could hold back her tears until he had gone. He took a few steps to the door, then to her complete distress he turned and came back again. Swiftly, he bent down and took her hand.

"Alys," he said gently, "I wasn't joking, my dear, believe me."

He put his fingers under her chin and made her look into his eyes. Her heart leapt as, through a mist of tears, she saw the look in his eyes. His gaze flicked over her features, and he shook his head gently, then drew her face towards him and, with infinite tenderness, brought his lips down on hers.

Alys closed her eyes wanting the long, precious moment to last to eternity, feeling indeed as if time was suspended, as if she were floating in space.

After a moment he looked into her eyes again. "I love you, Alys. I've never been so serious about anything in my life."

She still couldn't believe it. "Richard, why didn't you tell me before?" she asked in a bewildered fashion.

He grinned. "Are you still bent on sending me away? Or are you going to let me stay and try to explain to you?"

"Stay, Richard," she said simply.

He held out his hands to her. "Come and sit over on the settee beside me. I've a long tale to tell, and much as I like kneeling at your feet, it's giving me cramp."

She put both her hands in his, laughing up at him, and he pulled her to her feet. On the wide, comfortable settee he made no bones about putting his arm about her and resting her head against him.

"Are you sitting comfortably?" he recited. "Then I'll begin. For one thing, my dear Alys, until thi afternoon when I met Sister Halesworth, I thought you were engaged to Chalmers. You were supposed to be. Remember?"

"That was nothing more than a rumour put about by Olivia," she told him indignantly. "And you jumped to conclusions yourself."

"That only shows how consumed with jealousy I was," he murmured, his lips caressing her ear.

Ripples of happiness coursed up and down her spine, but she felt something more than her acquaintance with Ben or of their rumoured engagement had kept Richard away from her.

"You'll have to do better than that, Dr. Kent," she teased. "I never saw any signs of jealousy. You took Olivia out, and everybody thinks there's an 'understanding' between you."

He laughed. "There's an understanding all right—but not the kind you mean. No, to tell you the honest truth, my darling, I've loved you almost from the first day I met you, but I was afraid to let myself even dream about you. Oh, how I loved you, and how I loved teasing you! Then I thought I'd do something about it, only to realize that what I'd shied away from in the beginning was confirmed."

He paused absently, and fondled her ear. Alys remembered how he had looked at her the first time they had met at the station. What was it he had shied away from?

"Richard, do explain. I don't know what on earth you're talking about."

"It was your background, darling. That fur coat you were wearing and the way you wore it. Then when I met your father—well, obviously he's very wealthy."

Alys closed her eyes and braced herself for a blow. Was he trying to say that he would never marry her?

"I—don't take money from my father, Richard. I've

been independent since the day I took up nursing."

"My dear, I know. It was my stupid pride. I wanted to be able to give you all the things you'd obviously been used to—and more. I thought the best thing I could do was nip this thing in the bud. I told myself you were keen on Chalmers anyway, and—tried to forget you."

"By taking out Olivia?"

"Only once or twice. In fact, the other night I met her by accident and she virtually asked me to have a meal with her. I was glad of the opportunity to tell her what I thought of her, anyway, outside of the hospital. I never believed for a moment that you'd had anything to do with her wretched earrings, or any of the other petty thefts in the Home. I wanted an opportunity of telling her so. You know, you were pretty wonderful over that business. Sister Halesworth told me how you'd helped her. There's only one thing I want to know now."

Alys raised her eyes to his. "What's that?"

"What do you think?" he murmured. "Here am I, pouring my heart out to you. How do I know that you're even interested, that you care one little jot about me?"

She blinked. Then she smiled wickedly. "I've half a mind to keep you guessing. Besides—"

He gathered her to him. "Besides, what?" he murmured, his eyes scanning her face longingly.

"If you don't want to marry me—"

"Don't want to marry you?" he echoed. "I'm determined to now, in spite of your wealth. I must. I can't go on living otherwise. Alys, you will marry me, won't you?" he asked with sudden urgency.

She nodded. "Oh, Richard, I love you—"

For a second or two he gazed at her as if letting her words sink into his brain.

"Say that again, will you, darling?" he breathed.

But before she could frame the words his kisses were on her lips with that mixture of passion and tenderness which every woman longs for. Alys closed her eyes as a great sense of happiness and rightness settled into every fibre of her being.